Bound by Chains and Sashes

James Franklyn Jackson   2014 All Rights Reserved

The rights of James Franklyn Jackson © ___ to be i(
been asserted in accordance with the Copyright, De

Spiderwize
Remus House
Coltsfoot Drive
Woodston
Peterborough
PE2 9BF

www.spiderwize.com

J. Olive.
Best Wishes
James Franklyn Jackson
jfj112@hotmail.com

ACKNOWLEDGMENTS

This book would not have been possible without the patience and support of Patricia Irene Stevenson.

ODE TO MAYORALTY

(with apologies to Petrarch)

When you honoured me as your elected mayor
I pledged to represent you, one and all
And be at your constant beck and call
In a manner both transparent and fair
Despite political consensus being comparatively rare.
I found the determination and wherewithal
When speaking on issues, to be right on the ball
And when making decisions, I dared to dare.
Proudly wearing the gold chain and gown
With a clear mandate to improve your lot
I took up my duties at your behest
As first representative of our historic town.
I hope you were satisfied with what you got
You can't please all but I gave it my best.

Dorothy-Jane Woodfull
Mayor of Trenton Friars Town Council 1998

BOUND BY CHAINS AND SASHES

CONTENTS

Friendly French mayor with sash

INTRODUCTION

In the United Kingdom, it is often said that here is no one so forlorn as an ex-mayor. Gone at one fell swoop are all the trappings of privilege and power. No official chain of office, robes, secretary, chauffeur, mayoral limousine, private parlour or mayoral allowance. Invitations to glamorous functions a thing of the past. From first citizen of a city, town or village community, summarily voted out of office or relegated back to the ranks with drastically reduced ability to impose one's will on proceedings, influence or control others.

The recent introduction in some cities of publicly elected, highly paid mayors for a term of years has seen the position become highly politicised and regarded as a stepping stone to even greater positions of power.

However, several thousand communities still retain the title 'Mayor' for their first representative. Chosen by and from the body of elected councillors and assisted by a deputy, mayoralty is for a term of one year. There is no salary, but an allowance towards costs such as clothing, charity donations, stationery and civic hospitality. The position is largely ceremonial but behind the obvious glamour of wearing impressive civic regalia, duties carry serious and demanding responsibilities.
Mayoral attire is striking, dating back to the Middle Ages. Generally comprising of a fur lined red robe and black-feathered tricorn hat, an elaborate, heavy gold chain of office completes the outfit. Naturally, this gives rise to the holder being known as a member of 'the chain gang'.

In keeping with tradition, the first representative is addressed as either 'Mr Mayor' or 'Madam Mayor'. The wife of 'Mr Mayor' is 'Lady Mayoress', whereas the husband of 'Madam Mayor' is her 'Consort'. The mayor of a major city is titled 'Lord Mayor' as conferred by letters patent.

In Europe, ceremonially, there is often not so much instant pageantry associated with the office. The simple tri-colour sash with a gold tassel at the end, worn diagonally across the shoulder is less impressive as a symbol of authority and often worn over comfortable, casual clothes.

France, with over 38,000 municipalities, has a mayoral representative (*maire*) from the largest town to the smallest community.

Maires are paid, ranging from the six figure sums per year for *maires* of principal towns to just a few hundred euros for the *maire* of a small community. In larger towns, the *maire* is assisted by a number of elected deputies (*adjoints*) who are also entitled to wear the tri-colour sash, and members drawn from predetermined lists. It is customary to address a man as '*Monsieur le Maire*' and a lady as '*Madame le Maire*'.

Spain has more than 8,000 municipalities. The governing body is composed of a mayor (*alcalde* or *alcaldesa*) in Spanish, (*alkatea*) in Basque, aided by deputy mayors and an assembly of councillors.

Being elected for up to six years, European and the new breed of United Kingdom mayors become established in post. This can lead to vicious campaigns designed at retaining status at all costs.
Behind the scenes of these longer-term appointments, intrigue, bribery and corruption in one form or another are never far from the surface as powerful political machines try to dominate proceedings.

Many mayors are natural leaders. Occasionally however, due to political expediency, the role throws a compromise candidate into the limelight from virtual obscurity. Whatever the circumstances, very few fail to serve their full term of office and most are reluctant to relinquish it despite the pressures and demands upon their time.
This collection of short stories based upon true circumstances records the various styles, complexities and organization or, as many might conclude, disorganisation of the mayoral role in European cities, towns and village communities.

The first story is from Wales, followed by six from England.

'*The Mayor's Chauffeur*' relates the story of an experienced, overbearing chauffeur and his fraught relationships with successive mayors of the borough. On a Royal Garden Party visit, a battle of power ensues with a determined Welsh lady mayor that helps determine the chauffeur's future.

On to England where a justly proud mayor of the borough extols the attractions and delights of her seaside town as a conference resort in '*A Life of Riley*'. Some delegates however find the venue and services less than satisfactory whereas others discover the hidden pleasures very much to their liking.

Despite encouragement from the town's mayor, chief executive and a vivacious American girl, '*Gone for A. Burton*', is a sorrowful tale of misplaced influence, internal rivalry, over promotion and confirmation that 'still waters run deep'.

Only through the 'good offices' of the Lord Mayor did maladjusted teenager Donald Partridge find employment. As '*The Town Clerk's Clerk*', this gifted but social misfit yields to temptation after almost half a century of service, but with sympathetic support from his employer survives, eventually to receive an hitherto undisclosed fortune.

'*Amateur Dramatics*' finds the town mayor performing one of many necessary social functions – presentation of an award to a local worthy for an outstanding performance. The outcome was certainly not part of the original plot.

In '*Obsession*', the deputy chief executive's lifestyle of drink and sexual pre-occupation alienates the mayor, councillors and his principal. He manages successfully to pull a few strings to help the young girl with whom he is infatuated, but who pulled the string that ended his misery?

In the final story from England, automatic selection of mayor under the system known as '*Buggin's turn*', that has served the town so well for centuries, is challenged. It is eventually replaced but not before the deserving and courageous mayor in waiting, faced by enemies from within, decides to go it alone to win the day.

To Spain next and the story '*Town Twinning Farce*'. International and cultural differences turn celebration of the fiftieth anniversary into open conflict. The frustrated mayor of a Basque seaside resort has his work cut out when his conniving English counterpart runs riot and threatens to overturn the carefully nurtured friendship link in just a few short days.

In *'Tim's Sausages'*, the first of five French stories, a rural mayor, after decades of watching his village succumb to the lure of urban life, finds the arrival of an Englishman brings unexpected benefits. With renewed vigour, he embarks upon an unwitting plan of rural regeneration and receives the kudos so long denied him.

The enthusiasm of a newly elected mayor reaps reward for the long-suffering and out of pocket Rene Finot. A rejuvenated widow inadvertently obstructs an ambitious tycoon in *'The Viager'*, a French story of a property pledge that is a gamble in more ways than one.

A chance purchase by the town mayor has a profound effect upon the career of Jacques Grandcloud and his relationship with lifelong friend, Charles Cobert. *'The Portrait'*, also alludes to the public's view of the art world and the differing values they place upon it.

'Remembering Maslow', is an account of how, when all else fails, a word in the ear of the mayor can help overcome inertia and swiftly cut through the jungle of administrative red tape.

In the final story, *'The Tale of 'THE RAT''*, stop at nothing tactics result in an election impasse. Fierce rivalry, incompetence, corruption and legal wrangling are all in evidence as a fight to become town mayor discredits the democratic process.

Elected either directly by the public or chosen from an assembly of councillors from one of their number, it is usual for the elected person to pronounce: -

"I am proud to have been selected and fully accept the responsibilities you have bestowed upon me. I pledge to carry out my duties with complete integrity and will represent the interests of all inhabitants, not just those who voted for me."

After reading these short stories, you can judge for yourself whether or not these hopes and aspirations have been achieved.

If you are dissatisfied with your local administration, think you could improve accountability and have long held an ambition to be mayor of your community, be prepared. Local government needs people like you and one day, if you can remain true to your principles, you may get the chance to make a difference. Good luck!

THE MAYOR'S CHAUFFEUR

It was 11.30 in the evening. Edna Flynn's husband Bill had retired to bed leaving Edna to settle back in her favourite armchair, a glass of wine in hand.

Edna was approaching sixty-five and been married to Bill for over forty years. She had been a schoolteacher until retirement at sixty and a long time local councillor for her small Welsh village. People had said that she would miss teaching but she was full of life, had an abundance of ideas and was adept at carrying them out. Her council activities had more than compensated for the loss of school duties. A tireless worker, she had exchanged her teaching role for one of public duty, support for good causes and charity work. Bill was of North Walian farming stock, having inherited the estate from his father. He and Edna lived in the large farmhouse surrounded by five hundred acres of rich farmland. They had no children and consequently lived a hard working but comfortable lifestyle. Bill was the quiet dependable type whereas Edna was the go-getter. Once she had set her mind upon something she would stop nothing short of total achievement. When all the villages were given targets to raise money towards some charitable cause, it was invariably Edna's village that was first to reach its goal.

Edna was a small plump woman but deceptively energetic. Behind her short, curly dark hair, round face and horn rimmed glasses was a very sharp mind. She was an excellent motivator, her ideas and suggestions infectious. To achieve her goals, she regularly recruited help from people she felt appreciated her objectives and who were considered trustworthy. Once approached by Edna, it was impossible to say 'no'. Her heart was in the right place and she galvanised people into becoming an indispensable part of her team. One such person was the Borough Treasurer, Peter Goodhouse. She had cajoled Peter into assisting her to raise funds towards the cost of a body scanner at the city hospital seventy miles away. Peter had spent many evenings and weekends assisting at country fairs, selling raffle tickets, accounting for and banking numerous collections for the cause.

It was now mid July and as she drank her wine, Edna recalled what had happened so far during the year. She had started the year as deputy mayor of the council. That was a time of learning and preparation for her duties during her period of office as last mayor of the borough before reorganisation. In April, she had been fitted for her official robes - an ermine trimmed red velvet gown and a large tricorn hat. At the start of May, she had assumed the office of mayor at a solemn ceremony, with husband Bill as her consort.

Edna's secretary had informed her that during the year, the mayor of the borough generally undertook about seven hundred representative calls of duty. They ranged from official council meetings, church services, opening fêtes, welcoming visitors to tea in the mayor's parlour, presentations to worthy citizens and school prize giving events.

The one she cherished most of all referred to the letter she held in her hand - the annual mayoral invitation to Buckingham Palace garden party to which the mayor was allowed to invite two personal guests. Edna and Bill's first language was Welsh. Admirers of the Prince of Wales, they were fervent royalists and wanted a couple with whom they could share this memorable occasion. There were a number of friends Edna could have invited, but that week the target for the body scanner appeal had been achieved in record time. Edna had no doubts Peter Goodhouse and his wife were the couple she would invite. Upon forthcoming reorganisation, Peter was due to retire. Edna felt that the visit would be a just reward for his support and friendship during their council association.

The first quarter of the mayoral year had been a great success - hard work, tiring but very satisfying. There had proven to be much more to the job than she had realised. Having indefatigable energy and a sense of occasion, she had coped well with the challenges, becoming a popular mayor and representative of the borough.

There was just one small cloud on the horizon in what was otherwise a clear blue sky. It needed to be addressed but Edna was confident that she could deal with it successfully.

The role of mayor was also supported by provision of a mayoral car - a smart black, six seat Mercedes complete with mayoral pennant, together with a full-time chauffeur.

This had been the system for many years. Successive mayor's had availed themselves of this facility and thought highly of it. During times of financial cutbacks any suggestion that the mayor's car and chauffeur be axed was overwhelmingly defeated. The dignity of the borough and the mayor was priority and viewed as almost sacrosanct. The post of mayor's chauffeur had certain estimation. A uniform and peak cap was provided and the incumbent daily drove one of the most luxurious cars in town.

The present chauffeur, Ronald O'Day was a former regular in the army having attained the rank of sergeant. Upon retirement, he had been advised by his commanding officer to go back into civilian life and obtain the best job he could, as he was trained for and capable of doing almost anything. However, as a man in his mid-forties with few qualifications, the open market place had not proved to be the straightforward matter of walking into any job to which he thought he had a divine right. Eventually, he had lowered his sights and following a long line of military trained personnel, was appointed mayor's chauffeur.

He had been in post for five years and served five quite different types of mayor. A tall, slim handsome man who walked briskly with a swagger, he exuded an air of complete confidence. Having quickly obtained a feel for the job, the first three months of each mayoral year passed without incident. Ronald O'Day always assured a newly installed mayor that if a problem should arise to leave it to him, as he would always have a solution.

The mayor initially relied very much upon the organisational ability of the chauffeur. It was taken for granted that there would be a close working repartee between the two but as first citizen of the borough, the mayor must be totally respected. The trouble with Ronald O'Day was that his ego frequently got the better of him. An incoming mayor was subjected to the same treatment -"Yes Mr/Madam Mayor, leave everything to me." And they did until eventually they became aware of his foibles.

At first it was just small things. An afternoon function would end earlier than expected but the mayoral car was nowhere to be seen. It could have been located in the golf course car park awaiting Ronald to finish a few practice holes. Ronald would return to find the mayor waiting forlornly outside the premises. Instead of being embarrassed he would explain that he had just been to the local supermarket to buy stock for the mayor's parlour, carefully omitting to mention his bag of golf clubs and personal shopping in the boot. At other times, when a function was likely to continue into the early hours, he would request the mayor to be ready to leave early as one of his children had an important examination next day and he wished to return home by midnight. Occasionally he would arrive late with the Mercedes and then drive recklessly to the destination, giving the mayor palpitations. He had a short fuse. If things did not go according to his way of thinking he would become aggressive and thoroughly objectionable. If he could not park the car as close as possible to the entrance door at a function, he would jump out and demand to know whose car was blocking the way and upon finding the 'culprit', insist they move it! As the mayoral year progressed, Ronald O'Day increasingly acted as though he was more important than the mayor.

Edna Flynn was aware of possible trouble ahead. For the trip to Buckingham Palace garden party, she determined to leave nothing to chance. The previous year's mayor had told her how she had incurred Ronald O'Day's wrath when, after telling him that she had packed everything necessary for a town twinning visit to France, she had had to admit at a coffee break two hours later that she had left her passport she thought, on her kitchen table. Seething with rage, Ronald had quickly marched back to the car, returned to the mayor's house only to find that the 'missing' passport was not on the kitchen table but nestling all the time in the bottom of the mayor's large handbag. The poor lady was an eighty-two year old widow, kind and gentle but apt to forget. Ronald O'Day eventually reached Calais just in time for the ferry after breaking just about every motorway speed record. Everyone had laughed at the incident agreeing that in many ways, Ronald O'Day had got what he deserved.

By tradition, the Buckingham Palace garden party was always a four-day event with three nights half-board at the Rawlinson Hotel, situated not far from the Palace. The mayor's secretary had already booked the hotel and told the mayor that everything else would be taken care of by the chauffeur. He had already been given £1,200 for expenses, including provision of a picnic lunch before the afternoon garden party and tickets for a West End show.

On Tuesday morning, Ronald O'Day arrived promptly at the homes of both couples and drove them down to London without incident. They arrived at their hotel by mid-afternoon. After taking their cases from the car boot, Ronald informed them that he had parked the Mercedes in a rear car park. Their dinner was booked for 7.30 pm. He would be staying at a small hotel nearby with some of the other chauffeurs and would meet them after breakfast to discuss the day's itinerary.

Edna and Bill decided to lie in and miss breakfast and it was Peter who met a grinning Ronald O'Day in the foyer. He was holding a parking ticket issued by Westminster City Council.

"Damned cheek," he said laughingly."Last night I parked the car behind the hotel and put £10 in a machine for overnight parking. This morning, I checked the car and found this parking fine ticket for £50 attached to the windscreen wiper. I was able to trace the parking warden who turned out to be a smart, efficient young woman. She told me that overnight parking only lasted until 7.30 am and as it was 8 am when she had checked the car, she had issued a fine. I told her that she must have made a mistake and didn't she realise that it was the mayor's car being used for an important visit to the Palace? I gave her £5 and she promised she would cancel the ticket. You have to know how to handle things like that. Anyway, everything was settled amicably. Tell madam mayor that I am going to buy food for tomorrows picnic and I shall pick you up well in time for the 7.45 show this evening. Your buffet dinner is booked for 6 pm."

Ronald O'Day arrived at 7 pm for the short journey to the theatre but was delayed by heavy traffic in pouring rain. He became frustrated, thrust the tickets into Edna's hand and insisted that everyone must get out and walk the rest of the way to the theatre. To add insult to injury, the show had started at 7.30 pm and they had to apologetically take their seats with damp clothes a quarter of an hour late. On leaving the theatre, the rain continued to pour and they were grateful to see Ronald O'Day waiting outside with umbrellas. He ushered them to the Mercedes and went to such lengths to explain how difficult it had been to find a convenient parking place that the mayor congratulated him upon his initiative. "It's a good job we have Ronald to rely upon," she had said, tactfully.

Thursday was the day of the 3 pm garden party. Fortunately the rain had ceased when Ronald picked them up, dressed in all their finery, at the unusually early time of 11 am. Unbeknown to Edna, Ronald, by now on his sixth visit to the palace, regarded himself as the doyen of the chauffeuring fraternity. Not only was he in his opinion by far and away the best chauffeur, but also he drove the best car, represented the foremost borough and was chaperone to the most influential mayor and entourage. To confirm his status, he saw it as essential that his car, containing his mayor be first in the line of vehicles stationed in Green Park. He had decided upon this after his first visit and ever since had been head of the queue. Today was to be no exception and when he drove into the avenue of Green Park, showing his official identity card, he asked the security guard to confirm that his was the first vehicle to arrive and was delighted to hear that this was indeed so.

There was a long wait until the second vehicle arrived, followed shortly by many others. During this time, on the grass just inside the park, Ronald had been concentrating upon preparations for lunch. As he set up a table and four chairs, other chauffeurs greeted him cheerily, 'see you beat us to pole position again'.

After placing a cloth, napkins, glasses, knives and forks on the table, he produced a large hamper purchased from Fortnum and Masons. This was accompanied by two bottles of best champagne and a generous number of bottles of wine.

"Nothing but the best for our mayor and borough," he said gleefully as he poured them a glass of champagne, toasted their health and invited them to help themselves whilst he went to talk with the other chauffeurs.

There was so much food in the hamper, including fois gras, crab, lobster, quails eggs, ham, salad, a large selection of cheeses and pastries. Bearing in mind that they had enjoyed a hearty breakfast and were conscious of the forthcoming garden party fare, there was far too much to eat and drink. By the time they were satisfied, they felt that they had done scant justice to such a fine spread.

Ronald arrived back at 2.15 pm and packed everything away in the boot. He escorted them to the queue that had formed from the eight thousand invited guests and said he would be waiting for them when the garden party was over.

After that sumptuous lunch, it was a struggle for Edna and her party to eat the afternoon tea provided. At the end of a memorable occasion they returned to Green Park to find Ronald O'Day in relaxed mood. He was in high spirits, which they thought was due to his pre-eminent role as first among equals in the chauffeuring world.

"You can't beat an occasion like this," he enthused. "Now I'll run you back to the hotel where you will have plenty of time to change and relax before dinner."

"Dinner?" they all cried in unison. "After what we have eaten today, we couldn't face another large meal."

Peter had read in the morning paper that there was an evening race meeting at Sandown Park and being an enthusiast suggested to Ronald that he drive them all down there and that if they became hungry, they could continue on the unfinished hamper.

Ronald's mood changed abruptly. Flexibility was not his forte. He was used to giving instructions on a Buckingham Palace garden party visit, not being told what to do. He was also acutely embarrassed and wished to avoid being held to account. To maintain his position as the best and most fortunate chauffeur in the land, he had invited, as custom now had it, several other chauffeurs to join him in sampling the remaining contents of the hamper. Every morsel had been consumed and every drop of champagne and wine drunk. No wonder he was initially in high spirits!

Now he gritted his teeth and realised that he had to do some quick thinking.

"That's a wonderful suggestion but I'm afraid its just not possible Madam Mayor," he said turning towards Edna for support. "You see, I have already asked the hotel manager to reserve the best table in the restaurant for you and have ordered two bottles of their excellent wine. He knows that the Mayor always eats in his restaurant as an honoured guest and it would be embarrassing to Madam Mayor and insulting to the hotel manager if we were to cancel, don't you agree Madam Mayor?" he fawned ingratiatingly.

Edna could only but agree, suggesting that if they were not able to eat a full meal they could at least enjoy the wine.

Next morning, Ronald O'Day, having booked lunch at a restaurant in the Midlands, arrived as agreed at 10.30 for the journey home. To his consternation, he was given a message that the guests had gone shopping and would return in due course. Shortly after breakfast, it was Edna's idea that to acknowledge Ronald O'Day's organisational skills, they should club together to buy him a memento of the visit. Although Peter and his wife were not in total agreement with the idea, they were not disposed to argue the point.

Peter had already been surprised when, returning his room key to the front desk, the receptionist had presented him with the hotel bill. He had been given to understand that everything had been taken care of but to avoid delay had paid the large sum demanded with his own personal credit card, thinking he would recover it from the chauffeur. There didn't seem any hurry to depart and it shouldn't have taken long to find a suitable gift. Edna's shopping zeal hadn't been taken into account. After visiting several stores and discussing suitable gifts, it was noon when they returned having decided upon purchase of a golf sweater.

When they arrived back at the Rawlinson Hotel, Ronald was at his wits end. He had been forced to put more money into the parking meter and his lunchtime plans were in disarray. He hurriedly packed the suitcases into the car and drove as fast as he could out of London towards the Midlands. There was total silence in the back of the car as he cut corners on bends, put his foot down on the motorway and showed scant disregard to other road users on the very narrow lanes leading to the Midlands restaurant.

They arrived at 2.45 pm only to find that the chef was about to leave for home and that only sandwiches were available. If it hadn't have been for Bill, Ronald O'Day would have blown a fuse. Bill had been brought up to the simple life and had already eaten and drunk too much rich food and champagne.

"All I want Ronald," he said slowly, " is a cheese and pickle sandwich and a pint of beer." A snack satisfied them all and frayed tempers were calmed. Edna presented Ronald with his golf sweater and they returned home to North Wales without further incident. Later the following week, three parking fine tickets from Westminster City Council landed on Peter's desk. They were each for £50 for the previous Tuesday, Wednesday and Thursday nights. Also in the mail was a speeding ticket for the Mercedes, clocked at 115 miles per hour on the motorway the previous Friday afternoon. Peter called Ronald O'Day to his office.

"You told me that you had arranged to have your first parking fine ticket withdrawn and you didn't say anything about further tickets. Also we have this speeding fine," Peter commenced, waving the ticket under Ronald's nose.

Ronald cut in quickly. "That's the luck of the draw Boss," he replied, "some you win and some you lose. The ticket warden seemed a genuine lady and if she said she would cancel the fine, I would have expected her to do so."

"Ronald, you're a most unconvincing liar," retorted Peter. "It's only you who said you had paid her to withdraw the ticket. Obviously you didn't and she hasn't."

"Look Boss," pleaded Ronald, "everyone had a good time and all we are doing is arguing over a few pounds."

"A few pounds?" queried Peter. "Let's account for your expenditure. You were given £1,200 for expenses. What did you spend it on?"

"I'm out of pocket," said Ronald indignantly. "Things don't come cheap in London. I had three nights accommodation at £125 per night. Then there was the hamper, top quality as befits our mayor at a cost of £375, plus four bottles of champagne at £60 each and six bottles of wine totalling £120. Take account of car parking at £10 a night and various tips and oh yes, I almost forgot, four theatre tickets at £50 each and of course my personal expenses."

"You have also forgotten to add the parking fines and speeding ticket totalling over £200," added Peter sarcastically. "Why on earth you needed to buy such an expensive hamper for just four people is beyond belief. It is totally wasteful."

"But it's tradition Boss and we deserve it," replied Ronald. "It's always been like that."

"Well, it won't be in future," retorted Peter. "I was told that all the expenses were taken care of but when I was asked to pay the hotel bill plus meals and drinks it came to over £1,500. Supporting the Nation and representing the Borough is one thing but spending such a huge sum is a scandal."

"Well, you can claim it back like I intend to do," said Ronald vehemently.

"Lets be clear on this shall we Ronald. There will be no claiming back. You have had your £1,200 and whatever you did with the remaining hamper and drinks. The rest, including fines, will come from your salary. If it were to be seen that I had claimed back £1,500, I would be accused of exceeding my authority, abuse of public funds and would lose my job. I have sacked people for much less than that."

"But Boss, this has been happening for years and no one has ever said anything. I'm entitled to cover my expenses," pleaded Ronald O'Day.

"It doesn't necessarily follow that what happened in the past will always be continued. You've heard my decision. It's been costly for both of us but if you wish to appeal against it, that will be for you to decide, but don't expect me to support you," concluded Peter.

Ronald O'Day stormed out of the office. He knew that he had carried out his duties to the full, gone out of his way to ensure everyone had enjoyed the special occasion but was now being treated like a common criminal. He couldn't accept the decision. Did they not realise how much time the job required him to spend just waiting around for the mayor? The hours were unsociable for which there was no additional pay.

Was there no recognition or thanks for the numerous times he had saved the borough and its first representative from embarrassment and disgrace? Had he not on one occasion come between the borough's mayor who, worse for drink, was shouting at and fighting with his opposite number on a twinning visit? Or when he had broken up an altercation between an aggressive, womanising mayor and his jealous lady mayoress outside a high-class hotel at three in the morning? Where was the justice?

That afternoon, he was due to take the Mayor to a charity fête. When Edna remarked upon how much she had enjoyed the garden party, he couldn't resist telling her the tale of his financial woes. Next morning, Peter Goodhouse was summoned to the Mayor's parlour. Edna was in fine form as usual and asked him to take a seat.

"Just a couple of small but important matters to attend to," she said briskly. "First of all, I didn't realise that my secretary hadn't arranged to pay the London hotel bill. That was due to come out of my mayoral allowance," she said, " so here is my cheque in full reimbursement. Secondly, and I know it's against your wishes, I have also personally reimbursed Ronald O'Day his out of pocket expenses and will pay his car fines also. Now before you say anything, let me explain. You are right about the excessive cost of sending representatives to the garden party. The Mayor of the adjoining borough told me that he and his wife went to London by train, stayed at a small hotel overnight and came back next evening. Their trip cost £500, ours over £3,000. As you know, we will be amalgamated with that borough next April. As it is twice our size, they will have controlling representation. I have already been told that future mayoral visits to the garden party will be scaled down, so we should retain happy memories of our trip that we did in considerable style. You may think that I am being soft on Ronald O'Day but I am aware of his explosive nature and intend to ensure that he does not spoil the remainder of my mayoral year. He doesn't know yet, but I have also been informed by councillors who are likely to be elected to our successor authority that they do not support the funding of a mayoral car and chauffeur. Ronald O'Day will be made redundant and the new council will hire official cars as and when necessary."

In the event, the shadow council to the successor authority decided to dispense with the post of mayor's chauffeur and Ronald O'Day told that he would be made redundant but that a suitable alternative might be available to him. Under the procedure of 'slotting in', the shadow council had power to determine that existing officers be appointed to appropriate posts without formal interview.

In February, Ronald received a letter informing him that under the procedure, the shadow council was pleased to offer him the post of refuse collection driver with the new authority and asked him to confirm his acceptance as soon as possible. Faced with such humiliation, he immediately considered the small redundancy package on offer but realised that it was insufficient for his needs. He sought further posts without success. Eventually, swallowing his pride, he accepted the offer, swapping his smart uniform and peaked cap for overalls and flat cap. His days of heading the queue at Green Park in his Mercedes were replaced by lining up in his refuse vehicle to dump rubbish at the local tip.

Oddly enough, he soon found the early morning start and midday finish very much to his liking and the pay with bonus and occasional overtime far more remunerative. Having most afternoons free, by the end of summer he had acquired a healthy sun tan from his time on the golf course and also reduced his handicap by five shots.

A LIFE OF RILEY

Sam Ashsted, Revenue Officer, District No 10 was the man many of his fellow colleagues relied upon to book accommodation at their Institute's annual conference. This year, there had been pressures at work and urgent family business to attend to but he knew deep down that he had simply let things slide. The conference was scheduled for the last week in September. It was now the first week in August and he had made no arrangements. A phone call from George Berry, his opposite number at District No 7 asking for details of where they were to stay had focussed his attention on this outstanding matter.

"I've received a few quotes George," he responded deceptively. "It's just a question of a bit more negotiation to obtain our usual rates."

The officers received a set daily conference sum. Sam was adept at finding good hotels where the rate was considerably lower than their allowance so that they had an ample supply of pocket money for general expenses. Money was received in advance, production of receipts was not required and no one ever considered repaying any surplus.

Conferences were important to them, being demanding due to tight schedules, requiring concentration and attention to detail to derive maximum information. Their working practices were constantly changing. Now, it was all about challenges, performance targets, computerised systems and presentational skills. On top of that, politicians insisted upon introducing more and more complex and often confusing legislation. Conferences were no jolly but seen as essential in helping to understand and implement best practices in a modern, highly skilled organisation.If during the week there was the occasional chance to socialise, have a round of golf, a free dinner or two with sponsors or several late night drinks at the bar, then that was the reward for such dedication to duty!

Sam reviewed the current position. The conference was to be held in the Pavilion Building in the seaside resort of Cardingwold. The Institute had been there five years previously and he knew the venue well. Last time he had booked everyone into the three-star St George Hotel which had excellent rooms, good food, a well-stocked bar, free parking facilities,was centrally located and most importantly of all, was very reasonably priced.

Sam had a copy of the resort's Hotel and Accommodation Guide. There being no reason why he should not start with the St George, he picked up the phone and dialled their number.

"Last week in September? Oh, sorry Sir, it's the conference season you know. Hotels get booked up well in advance and I'm afraid we are no exception. You could try the Ashville just down the road. I'll give you their number," answered the receptionist.

An hour later, Sam had tried ten different hotels without success. 'Perhaps I shall have to lower my sights a little this year,' he thought, turning to the 'Guest Houses' section. After a few abortive calls, he saw the smallest advertisement,

RILEY'S GARDEN RESIDENCE
CENTRAL, BAR, PARKING, CHEAP.

'Couldn't be more succinct and maybe worth a try at this late stage?' he wondered.

He phoned. After what seemed like an eternity, a bright, cheerful voice laughingly answered, "Alf Riley here. What can I do you for?"

"Ah, Mr Riley," replied Sam cautiously. "Do you have seven single rooms available during the last week in September, five nights bed and breakfast Sunday until Friday morning?"

Without seeming to think, Mr Riley responded, "Yes, no problem at all. It might be a tight squeeze but we'll fit you in alright."

"And the price?" Sam queried.

"£30 per head a night," chirped Mr Riley.

Expecting to pay considerably more, Sam jumped at the offer, giving Alf Riley his address and phone number, promising to post a deposit of £200 by return.

Next morning, he was able to contact the other six Revenue Officers to tell them the good news of the booking and the even better news of the price.

Late on that Sunday afternoon, Sam drove slowly around the centre of Cardingwold trying to locate 6, Rylands Terrace, the address given by Mr Riley. Sam had picked up George Berry and had driven leisurely through the countryside towards the coast, stopping for lunch on the way. The five other Revenue Officers had set out separately to drive to the guest-house. After passing by any number of smart hotels, Sam had to stop and ask a couple of pedestrians for directions. He was pointed towards what turned out to be a narrow street with prominent yellow 'no parking' lines. It contained a row of large, dingy six-story terraced properties. Opposite was a line of several dilapidated looking shops, one or two boarded up and clearly derelict. At the end was a large private underground car park. Sam decided to park temporarily on the uneven footpath outside No 6 whilst George got out to ask Mr Riley for directions to his car park. Mr Riley, a small, slim dark-haired man in his early thirties with a long pony tail and a large gold ring in his left ear, answered the door promptly. He told George that the underground car park across the road was where all the guests parked and that it was safe and convenient. He failed to mention, as Sam soon found out, that the cost of a weekly ticket was £60. As they trundled their heavy suitcases across the road, Mr Riley was waiting for them at the front door.

"Welcome to No 6," he enthused. "All your colleagues have arrived and are busy unpacking. I just need to know which of you is Mr Ashsted."

"That's me," said Sam.

"Then you're in room 11 but I'm afraid you won't be able to use the shower. The last guest made a crack in the plastic floor and room 9 below complained of water cascading onto the bed. Your friend here," continued Mr Riley, "will be in room 9 and you wouldn't want to inconvenience him so it's best if you arrange to take a shower in his room. It's very hard to get a plumber at short notice and the repair can't be done until next week. Now, if you go and unpack, I'll meet you later with your colleagues in the lounge on the first floor."

Twenty minutes later, a somewhat disillusioned Sam and George trooped into the lounge. There was no lift in the house and they had had great difficulty heaving their heavy suitcases up the steep, winding staircases. The rooms were small and drab with few of the facilities they had come to take for granted. There was no tea-making machine, television, trouser press, hair-drier, not even a picture or two on the walls. The sparse furnishings were old and worn.

Sam tried to lift the gloom, turning to Mr Riley, saying, "I think I'd better buy you all a drink. What's everybody's poison?"

"That's the spirit," replied Alf Riley cheerily. "You all tell me what you want and I'll arrange to get them for you." They indicated their preferences.

"So, it's three beers, two gin and tonics and two large whiskies," he counted.

"Can you tell me if you will require another round because my drinks licence hasn't come through yet and I'll have to go down to the local supermarket to buy some stock? Oh, and by the way, if you could pay me for them now and also tomorrow morning for the outstanding board and lodgings in cash, I'd be very much obliged. I do a lot of business here and like to keep on top of things."

When he had disappeared down the road, everyone turned towards Sam. "Just what sort of place have you booked us into?" they asked in unison. Only Arnold from District 13 could see the funny side of things.

He chortled, "I arrived here first and because of my recent hip operation asked for a ground floor room. Mr Riley told me that was not possible as both ground floor and cellar rooms were on long-term let to two ladies. When he carried my case up to room 3, I caught a glance of one of them and it didn't take too much imagination to realise what sort of business goes on around here! I also thought that the name 'Garden Residence' implied a restful outdoor space but when I said I would wait for you all in the garden, Mr Riley told me that although the old name remained, the former garden had been sold off for construction of private garages many years ago."

Sam had to admit that 'Riley's' did not appear to be one of his better bookings but even with car parking charges the rate was still low and to their advantage.

Next morning they all assembled in the lounge in anticipation of a hearty breakfast to fortify them for the long day ahead. There was no sign of Mr Riley, no sign of a dining room and no smell of cooking. It was one of the 'ladies', 'Doreen', as she introduced herself, casually attired in a plum coloured velvet dressing gown, who informed them that breakfast would be served at 'Franks Café' across the road. The cost would be £5 a head and they would be served what she described as "the best fry-up in town." "That's another £25 off our expenses," complained the delegates to Sam.

Returning to the guesthouse, Sam aired their complaints to Alf Riley who had arrived in the lounge dishevelled, appearing only just to have got out of bed.

"Come on, be fair," countered Alf. "I never advertised free parking or breakfast included but you have got the very cheap rate I offered. Also, the two young ladies on the ground floor, who have been a godsend to me since my wife walked out, will attend to your every need. You'll be perfectly happy here and will enjoy your conference. What's on the agenda today?" he asked, quickly changing the subject.

A chastened Sam meekly replied, "We always open with a welcome speech from the mayor followed by our Presidents speech. This year he's an interesting character called Ambrose Seaton, a Director of a bailiff firm called 'Recovery Investigations'.

"Recovery Investigations?" queried Alf Riley, his face registering surprise and alarm. "They were around here a few weeks ago. Nasty pieces of work they were. I had to pay them some money to go away. Later they returned and started to list all my furniture and effects. I paid a little bit more and they went away. I wouldn't like to get on the wrong side of them."

"Unfortunately many people do," replied Sam. "In our job, it's difficult to get some people or businesses to pay their rightful dues, so bailiffs are an essential part of our armoury," he continued, wondering just how much debt Mr Riley had accumulated.

The conference got off to a good start. The Mayor, a jovial lady wearing a smart, dark blue costume suit adorned by her imposing gold chain of office, said how delighted she was that the Institute had once again chosen her elegant and historic town to hold their conference. It was a pleasure to welcome them back and she was sure that once again they would fully enjoy the facilities the resort afforded to all its guests. Since their last visit, a new marina had been opened and for her last birthday, she had received the present of a small yacht from her husband. To much laughter, she informed delegates that she now had first hand experience of the old saying 'when your ship comes in it is always docked by the revenue collectors'. She wished them a successful conference and handed the microphone across to the Institute's President.

Ambrose Seaton, a small thick-set man with distinguishing grey, wavy hair, moustache and neatly trimmed beard slowly rose to his feet. He thanked the Mayor and proceeded to gave an inspirational opening address, concluding that he was certain everyone would have a memorable week in Cardingwold.

If inclement weather put a slight damper on things, only Arnold in room 3 was disturbed from time-to-time by the goings-on in the cellar below. He looked out of his window several times and observed men either alighting from or returning to taxis and concluded that damp evenings were good for some trades.

By the end of the second day however, their numbers had been reduced to six.
Another delegate had told Douglas from District 14, that there was a vacancy at his excellent hotel. Walking back to 6 Rylands Terrace in pouring rain following the afternoon conference session, he had found Mr Riley stretched out on the lounge sofa, glass of wine in hand watching horse racing on the television. Retiring to his small, dark, damp and inhospitable room, he found that there was no hot water for a shower. Mr Riley blithely informed him that the immersion heater was not switched on until 6 pm and he would have to wait until then. Douglas immediately decided to cut his losses and transfer to more amenable, if expensive accommodation.
Sam later took the opportunity to transfer to the vacant room that, for all its shortcomings, did have a usable shower after 6 pm.
Everyone else had reluctantly complied with Doreen's advice to take their wet clothes to a nearby laundry service where she said, 'by next day they would be washed, dried, ironed, folded and in perfect condition. And all for such a reasonable cost'!
By Wednesday evening, they were down to three. Gerald and Robert, both suffering from irritable bites on their arms and legs that had turned into large, painful blisters decided to return home early, unconvinced by Doreen's assertion that the bed clothes were changed and washed each day.
"Maybe the sheets and pillowcases are but that blanket and old carpet haven't been cleaned for years," complained Gerald.
"And those curtains could open and close without any assistance," added Robert. They had been to a chemist shop and asked where they were

staying. When they had replied 'Rylands Terrace,' the pharmacist had regarded them in horror, sold them some ointment and ushered them out of his shop as quickly as possible.

David, having asked Alf Riley if he could provide a hairdryer had been given one with a very short flex. As the only available three-point socket was situated just above the hallway skirting board, David was only able to use it by crouching down and bending his head towards the floor in an undignified manner. He hadn't been amused when other guests had laughed at the sight of his backside sticking up in the air. He also managed to find alternative accommodation and moved without delay.

Along with Sam and George, only Arnold remained. Arnold felt honour bound to stay. On Wednesday evening, another damp, cold night, he had returned to Rylands Terrace early and encountered what he described as 'a young lady wearing a low-cut dress and short skirt'. She had approached him, asking in a friendly manner if they might do business. He had looked her up and down, said he was too old for that sort of thing and advised her to return indoors and put on an overcoat before she caught her death of cold. He then added gratefully, "but thank you all the same for asking me my dear."

Arnold later learned that the girl was Nora who occupied the other ground floor flat opposite Doreen and directly below his room number 3.

Alf Riley was in buoyant mood when they met him briefly before breakfast on Thursday morning as he was reading the 'Racing Post'. "Four down, three to go," he joked. "I hope you don't mind but even though your friends have paid for their rooms, they are now available for re-letting. I had a telephone call first thing from a gentleman who said he and two of his colleagues would like to come and see them this afternoon. So, when you return this evening there should be some new guests." Off he went whistling cheerfully, shouting across to Doreen that she and Nora had better give the rooms a bit of a clean.

As so often happens after a prolonged spell of poor weather, transformation is sudden and unexpected. Thursday had dawned bright and sunny; the sky was a clear blue and the rise in temperature promised a long pleasant day ahead.

Sam, George and Arnold ambled slowly along the road towards the promenade. The sea was calm at last. They enjoyed the light-cooling breeze and looked forward to the conference sessions ahead and the dinner that they had been invited to that evening.

When they arrived back at 6 Rylands Terrace at 6 pm they had been anticipating a cool shower, a change into their dinner suits and a welcome beer. What they encountered was an atmosphere approaching total chaos.

Alf Riley, Doreen and Nora were haranguing a man dressed in a black suit and tie with two younger men in tee shirt and jeans looking on menacingly.

Alf Riley was gesticulating frantically when suddenly he saw Sam and his two colleagues. He rushed over to him, pulling the man in the suit and tie along with him.

"This is Mr Ashsted. He knows what the likes of you are up to and the illegal tactics you employ," he shouted.

"What's all this about?" demanded Sam. "Who are these men Mr Riley?"

"They're the three men I told you about this morning. The said they wanted to view the vacant rooms. They tricked me into being here to show them around and then said they were bailiffs from 'Recovery Investigations'. They want to take all my furniture and ruin my business. They're just bullies and crooks. You tell them Mr Ashsted, you're a friend of their boss. Tell them that they can't just come in here and upset everyone with strong-arm tactics. I gave them money last time. They want more but I haven't got enough."

Sam quickly took control of the situation.

"I think you will find that if 'Recovery Investigations' have returned, they will have the necessary authority Mr Riley." The man in the suit and tie nodded, producing a legal warrant.

"If you cannot pay," continued Sam, "then they are entitled to take sufficient goods to satisfy the debt. It isn't they who are crooks Mr Riley, but you."

Turning to the bailiffs, he continued, "I propose we suspend operations for today. We are going to our rooms to shower and change for dinner. When we return Mr Riley, we expect to be treated as paying guests in this establishment not as a means for you to make easy money. All you seem to want to do is to lounge around all day and expect the world to provide you with a good living."

When they came down at 7.30 pm, the bailiffs had gone and there was no sign of Mr Riley, Doreen or Nora.

As a precaution against anything untoward happening, Sam, George and Arnold packed their suitcases and took them down to their cars.

After dinner, they returned to 6 Rylands Terrace by taxi not knowing what to expect.

"I wouldn't put it past an operator like Alf Riley to have changed the locks since we left," mused George.

"If that's the case, we shall have to transact some business with Doreen and Nora," guffawed Arnold. "The girls were doing a brisk trade earlier this evening. I didn't tell you but just before I came down to meet you, the hooting of a taxi horn and doors banging disturbed me. I looked down from my window and saw a short, grey-haired man leave Nora's cellar below and get in. If I'm not mistaken, I think he looked very much like Ambrose Seaton."

Fortunately, all was quiet and they were able to recover their suitcases from the cars and let themselves in. Having showered and changed early next morning they decided to give 'Franks Café' a miss. They checked out, leaving their keys on the lounge table and taking their suitcases back to the cars. They had a light breakfast at a café on the promenade, shortly afterwards taking their places at the final conference session to hear the President's closing speech.

They heard Ambrose Seaton thank the Mayor of Cardingwold for hosting their conference in the magnificent Pavilion Building, adding that he had no doubt every delegate had benefited from the excellent programme of events they had attended throughout the week. Cardingwold had set an example to all in the way the town was run, its citizens behaved and in the high-class accommodation provided. He was confident he spoke for everyone when he said it was a privilege for the Institute of Revenue Officers to have held their conference in the town. He was sure they would wish to return before very long to once again enjoy the many delights it offered.

Arnold decided to leave for home as soon as the conference ended but Sam and George stayed on for lunch with some of the other delegates on the veranda of the main conference hotel.

There, at an adjacent table overlooking the sea, they saw Alf Riley, Doreen and Nora, stylishly dressed, enjoying a bottle of wine and discussing the luncheon menu with a waiter.

Alf caught sight of them and came over with Nora.

"I don't think you have met Nora, Doreen's friend from Room 1. She's a very industrious girl and gets along very well with all of our many customers. This morning," he continued, " those bailiffs returned and said that their boss had instructed them to withdraw the distraint warrant. I owe you my thanks as it must have been your friendship with the top man that did the trick."

Sam looked somewhat puzzled until he saw the sly wink Nora directed towards him.

"I let them take away much of the old furniture to help cover their costs," continued Alf Riley. "They did us a favour really as it would have cost more to hire a van to transport that old stuff to the tip. Now the house is almost empty, we are going away for the winter. Rylands Terrace has been designated a General Improvement Area by the council and I'll qualify for generous refurbishment grants. After that I'm going to redecorate and re-stock with furnishings from an out of town furniture discount store. They offer long-term credit facilities for enterprises such as the 'girls' and mine. Next year, you'll find me under the 'Hotels' section of the guide. My weekly rate will be higher but for good regular customers such as you, I'll be able to offer a large discount for cash."

As he left with Nora to return to their table, they heard him shout, "Waiter, another bottle of your best wine for our table and one for my friend Mr Ashsted."

After the main course, Alf Riley shouted a farewell to Sam and George and left with the two girls in tow. Sam saw him in deep conversation with the manager at the check-out desk. Then, turning quickly with a swish of his pony tail, he gave them a last friendly wave and was gone.

"Phew, what a con-man," whistled Sam. "I don't want any more dealings with his type."

After the other delegates had departed, Sam and George enjoyed a final coffee and were last to leave. When Sam asked for their bill he winced when he saw the amount.

"This is a mistake," he complained to the waiter. "You have charged us for five lunches and three bottles of your expensive wine."

"I'll just check with the manager," replied the waiter tactfully.

After a brief conversation, the manager came to their table.

"Everything is correct," he informed them. "When those three friends of yours from the next table left a few minutes ago, the man gave me a small tip for the waiter and said that as they were part of your group, you would be paying the bill in full. I think you will find the £150 to be perfectly in order. Will payment be by cash or credit card?"

GONE FOR A. BURTON

Headley Carlton-May was not a man to be denied. All his life he had been able to get his own way and was determined not to be thwarted this time. Having made a decision he knew instinctively to be right, he was in no mood to taste defeat. To him, success was second nature.

Headley Carlton-May was born in 1908 in the South of England. In childhood, he had suffered from polio, as a result of which, he always walked awkwardly with a pronounced limp. A bright child, by the age of 24 he had gained his Bachelor of Law degree from Oxford and obtained a post in the Chief Executive's department of a large London Borough. He genuinely felt a sense of pride and privilege, knowing in that era, many people were unemployed and living in poverty. Working in London, he experienced the depression years, the emergence of extreme right wing organisations and the period leading up to the Second World War.

He was an odd sort of character. Standing just over five feet tall and weighing no more than nine stones, this slight figure none the less walked quickly with his uneven gait, shoulders firmly back, body stiff and upright. With his dark, thinning hair, thick black moustache, large protruding ears and uneven teeth, people meeting him for the first time were instantly reminded either of Will Hay's characterisation of Adolph Hitler in '*The Goose Steps Out,*' or Charlie Chaplin's impersonation in '*The Great Dictator.*' If had had known of these thoughts, he would have smiled for this was precisely how he operated.

He was also a talented linguist, fluent in German and French. In his early twenties, he visited both countries as often as he could to gain practical experience of the languages. With his military dictatorial appearance, rumour abounded that he had attended rallies whilst holidaying in Germany and that he was sympathetic to the Nazi cause, although there was no firm evidence of this. At the start of war, he had applied to join army intelligence but due to his physical deformity, was rejected.

He remained with the London Borough until just after the war, rising to the post of Senior Assistant Solicitor. He then applied for the post of Chief Executive of Fielden City Council in the North of England. Partly benefiting from the lack of experienced legal personnel at that time, he was appointed at the relatively early age of 38 and took up residence in the grand nineteenth century City Hall.

He decided from the outset that he would transform the day-to-day operations of the Council and introduce streamlined working practices. His dedication to the value of study and attainment of qualifications was derived from his formative years. He immediately decreed that the Council would encourage and financially support staff to train with a view to progression. His succession-planning programme was designed to ensure that there was always someone on hand trained and ready to take over when staff left for other posts or retired.

With this uppermost in his mind, he had upon reaching the age of 62, decided to ensure that when he retired in three years time, there would be an obvious internal candidate.

As head of the Management Team of Chief Officers, he had been able to assess at first hand the abilities and potential of those officers. There were some bright prospects, ambitious men and women whom he knew were eager to further their careers. He also knew that, as Chief Executive for what would then be 27 years, members of the Council would be sounding him out and seeking his advice.

After careful consideration, he had made the decision that his Deputy, Lawrence Shawcross, would be his successor.

Lawrence Shawcross had been appointed as Headley Carlton-May's deputy five years previously. Headley had been impressed by his background, which included several years in private practice. Headley himself had advised the interview panel that Shawcross was a candidate with whom he could work and one, in his view, who would best benefit the Council. No one dared to challenge Headley Carlton-May's opinions, especially on legal matters and Lawrence Shawcross had been selected. He was then 34 years of age, tall, slim clean-shaven, good looking in a boyish sort of way with long wavy dark hair and thick horned-rimmed spectacles. His wife, Hilary was an attractive brunette and a legal secretary. They were living in the West Country but having neither children nor ties, hadn't any qualms about moving North. In fact, they both welcomed the change and challenge of a move to a new environment.

Lawrence had quickly settled into his job. He was willing to learn from the dictatorial Headley Carlton-May and enjoyed getting to know the intricacies of local government legal work. Hilary's experience soon saw her appointed as legal secretary to a local firm of solicitors. With their joint salaries, they were able to arrange a mortgage to buy a house in a leafy suburb.

Gradually, Headley concentrated on dealing with chief officers, councillors and committee work, leaving the day-to-day running of the department to his deputy.

Lawrence threw himself into his work. He was a stickler for accuracy and took it upon himself to double check all letters and documents before they left the department. It made heavy demands upon his time leaving little for relaxation and enjoyment. Within four years, his marriage foundered and shortly afterwards, Hilary filed for divorce. Lawrence moved out of the matrimonial home into bed and breakfast accommodation. During the period of divorce proceedings, his work became an obsession. He was deeply affected by the split from Hilary. With no comfortable home to return to, he remained in the office until late in the evenings often stopping off at a fast food restaurant for a snack or a take-away meal. Eventually, the divorce was settled. With the exception of telling Headley Carlton-May and legal members of his staff that his marriage was over, he never referred to it again.

They had shared their assets equally but after repaying the mortgage and divorce legal fees, Lawrence had only a small sum of ready cash. A single child, his parents lived in the South of England and in due course he anticipated inheriting all their substantial assets. He decided that in his circumstances that a small modern apartment, that had become available to rent within a larger block close to City Hall, would be convenient for him. After supplying the necessary references and paying rent in advance, he signed the agreement. He was now the tenant of a third floor apartment, No 35.

With a place of his own, he was now able to enjoy a more comfortable, convenient lifestyle. Gradually, he decreased his late nights at the office. At first, it was hardly noticeable to Headley Carlton-May, but little-by-little it became clear that Lawrence's attention to detail was not what it was. There was the occasional lack of clarity in his legal drafts and even omissions, not too serious in themselves, but sufficient for Headley Carlton-May to have a quiet but firm word with him.

As the months went by, staff noticed that Lawrence had withdrawn into his shell. His office 'engaged' light was on for long periods. When eventually seen, he was difficult to communicate with, his natural shyness coming to the fore. He became apologetic for his shortcomings, especially when late for appointments. His colleagues could not help noticing that without a wife to support him, he was not as smart in appearance as they had come to expect. One of the secretaries had tactfully suggested that drip-dry shirts were a boon and at least he had taken that on board.

Headley Carlton-May was becoming a worried man. Never before in his life had he been proved wrong about the character and potential of an employee. Yet his protégé, Lawrence Shawcross, who he himself had chosen and promoted as his successor was proving to be a great disappointment. He determined to rectify the situation before it was too late.

The crisis came to a head just before Easter and provided Headley Carlton-May with the greatest challenge of his life, focussing his attention upon a very serious matter that he had not anticipated. It was the final Council Meeting before the May elections.

It should have been a straightforward meeting but a 'point of order' question arose which Headley delegated to Lawrence to answer. There was an obvious reply and Headley thought it would give Lawrence a chance to shine and impress. To Headley's embarrassment, Lawrence appeared flustered, his response was hesitant and the member who had raised the point was not satisfied with his reply.

"Perhaps Chief Executive, if your Deputy does not know the answer, maybe another of your officers does. What about the City Treasurer?" he suggested.

To Headley's horror, the City Treasurer Mr Arthur Burton had had the effrontery to reply, "Yes Sir, I think I may be able to assist in this matter," and had proceeded to defuse the problem by giving a succinct response that the member and full council had accepted without further debate.

Headley Carlton-May now knew that he had a fight on his hands.

Arthur Burton had been City Treasurer for three years, having successively been chief accountant and deputy city treasurer. His appointment as chief accountant from a neighbouring Borough was initially fraught with problems. By general consent, he was a first-class accountant but hyperactive and combustible. He lacked delegation skills, wishing to be involved in everything down to the merest detail. Arthur Burton's explosive nature often erupted in the open plan accountancy office. He showed members of staff no mercy, shouting at them in a loud excitable voice telling them exactly what he thought their faults were in front of the rest of the section. Such was the force of his voice that it reverberated around all the offices, so that everyone in the department knew that some poor soul was 'getting it in the neck'.

Arthur Burton was a short, well built individual with thick, slicked back black hair, fat drooping jowls and a pale anaemic looking skin. He was of smart appearance, usually with a dark, double- breasted suit, white shirt with matching tie and pocket-handkerchief. 'Rotweiller' was his sobriquet and all he lacked was a handler and a muzzle. Staff genuinely feared his temper. On occasions, he reduced the two female loans assistants to tears by going over their heads and arranging to borrow or repay loans without reference to them. Never did he issue an apology for his behaviour, not that he would ever have considered one necessary.

After only two years in post, staff had been amazed when Lionel Spedding, the newly promoted City Treasurer, appointed Arthur as his Deputy. It proved to be an astute move by Lionel. He had appreciated Arthur's talents as an accountant and the need to take him out of an open plan office and install him in his own room. Out of harms way of day-to-day operations, Lionel gave Arthur full reign in planning the strategy of the department and liaison with outside organisations. Dealing with people on or above his level of authority was the making of him. He matured quickly, learned the art of timing and tact in conversation and even developed a sense of humour rarely seen in the past.

Arthur had often crossed swords with the chief rating officer, Kingsley Spencer, a small dapper but timid man. Needless to say, their exchanges had reduced Kingsley to an apologetic simpering wreck, unable to combat Arthur's verbal assault. Now as deputy, Arthur had recounted to staff with some humour that recently whilst driving home 'some idiot' had cut across him at speed. When he had given the culprit a long blast on his horn, the driver had braked suddenly, turned, given him a 'V' sign and driven off 'like a boy racer'. He had recognised the driver as Kingsley Spencer. The thought of 63 years old Kingsley getting the better of Arthur and being described as a 'boy racer' greatly amused staff and did no harm to the standing of either.

Arthur's transformation in the treasurers department was complete when Lionel retired and he was promoted to City Treasurer.

Under his leadership the department was recognised as a very professional outfit and greatly respected. At departmental management team meetings, Headley Carlton-May had to admit that Arthur had developed into a fine manager whose opinion was often sought and acted upon. He still retained his combative temperament but was now able to control it and judge situations where use of his forcefulness would pay dividends. He was also ambitious and was now at a stage where he felt able to look to opportunities for advancement.

This was Headley Carlton-May's dilemma. With only four months to go before retirement, he was confronted by his protégé whose halo had fallen against a rival whose star continued to be in the ascendancy.

Immediately after Easter, Lawrence Shawcross was returning home to his apartment after another depressing day at the office. He had recently headed a council delegation to Strasbourg to press for European funding for a new sports centre. The application was well structured and within the terms and conditions for assistance. However, he had received feedback from accompanying councillors that his presentation had been lacklustre. That morning, a letter had been received stating that funding would be granted but on a scale much reduced from that requested. The council would have to go back to the drawing board. It was very disappointing and he knew he would have to bear the major responsibility for lack of success.

As he entered the lift and pressed button No3, a young woman dashed quickly in to join him. The doors closed. He looked across but did not recognise her thinking she must be visiting someone in the building. At the third floor, the door opened and he alighted, took out his key and went to open the door of No 35. He was not aware that the woman had followed him, but as he put the key into the lock, he heard her say, "Hi, you must be one of my neighbours. I've just moved into No 38 across the way." He turned to look at her. She was tall, late 20's, blond with impeccable make-up, very well dressed in a stylish long casual coat with a silk scarf expertly drawn around her neck. Before he could answer, she put out her hand, introducing herself as "Carolyn Fernandez from Texas." He shook her hand tentatively, finding himself mumbling "Yes, I've been here several months and oh, by the way, I'm Lawrence Shawcross."

"I'm really sorry Lawrence but I'm in a real hurry," she replied quickly, "have to be out again in half an hour. We must meet up sometime - nice to talk to you."

With that she went across to No 38, opened the door and went inside.

Lawrence's gloom was not sufficiently lifted for him to give her any further thought and a week went by without contact. One afternoon, he was walking across the foyer of City Hall towards a group of people mingling near the entrance. He saw Headley Carlton-May, the Mayor and some councillors amongst them and as he passed by was surprised to hear a woman's voice say "Hi," and a hand wave to him.

As Headley Carlton-May was talking to the group at the time, he merely nodded and walked on. He was in no doubt however that it was the newly arrived blond at No 38. Late that afternoon he received a call to go to the Chief Executive's office. Headley Carlton-May was busy pouring a double whisky and he also poured one for Lawrence. "Had a very busy afternoon Lawrence. A party from the university asked for a tour of City Hall. They are students of politics and wanted an insight into the workings of local government, so I also invited the Mayor and some of our councillors to attend. The students were very bright indeed, particularly that blond American girl. She asked many pertinent questions and impressed everyone. You didn't tell me you knew her Lawrence?"

"I don't really know her at all Chief Executive. I've only met her once. She has moved in across from my flat and that's all I can tell you," said Lawrence.

"Well," replied Headley, "take my advice Lawrence and have a word with that girl. She would do you a lot of good."

Lawrence did not need to have a word, for next evening there was a knock on his door and when he answered, Carolyn was standing there.

He invited her in, even though the apartment was not as tidy as he would have liked. He offered her a drink, but she refused.

"I've just called to say that I hadn't got the time to talk yesterday afternoon. Your Mr Headley Carlton-May is such a demanding host - kept us all on our toes for over two hours at City Hall but he was really interesting. He spent a lot of time telling us about the workings of your local elections answering all of our questions in a very informative way. Then, we had tea and biscuits in the Mayor's Parlour. The Mayor dressed in his fine red robe and wore his ancient chain of office for the occasion. He insisted I be photographed with him. It was a wonderful experience and so delightful for us to see at first hand your quaint English customs and traditions. Your lucky to be able to work in such a dynamic environment and to have such a talented man as Mr Headley Carlton-May as your chief," she gushed.

Heeding Headley's advice, Lawrence said that if she would like to know more about political life at Fielden City Council, perhaps they could meet for dinner one evening.

During the next month, they met once a week. Lawrence learned that Carolyn lived in Houston, Texas, having studied law and politics at university. She was now on secondment for a year at Fielden University to advance her knowledge of local government in the United Kingdom. "My flat is on a twelve months rental and I'm here to learn as much as I can," she told him."Mr Headley Carlton-May has already introduced me to some of your councillors and we are getting on real well. So, Lawrence," she stated firmly, "Mr Headley Carlton-May has mentioned that he is soon to retire, so does that mean you will become the next Chief Executive?"

True to Headley's comment, Carolyn proved to be as bright as he had said. She soon had Lawrence weighed up. Whilst he was likeable enough, for her, he didn't seem to have that spark she was sure was necessary. She had also received comments and coded messages from some councillors she had met as to Lawrence's fall from grace in his job.

It wasn't any of her business and it wouldn't have been if Lawrence, in a rare moment of assertiveness, had not invited her to accompany him to the Civic Ball the following Friday evening. It was traditional for this to be held the week after the local elections to celebrate the new Council and enable members and officers to socialise in an informal and pleasant atmosphere.

She was delighted to accept. For the occasion, Lawrence hired a dinner suit and looked very much the part. He was stunned when he went to pick up Carolyn across at No 38. She wore a very stylish, obviously expensive ball gown with matching silver necklace and earrings. By common consent, they were by far the best-dressed, most eye-catching couple of the evening. At dinner, Carolyn was seated next to Arthur Burton's wife Margaret. Margaret was a plump, dumpy woman, faithful and subservient to Arthur. In many ways, the pairing of Lawrence and Carolyn was similar. Carolyn was the 'socialite', an excellent intelligent conversationalist full of confidence. Lawrence was presentable but quiet, guarded, shy and backward at coming forward. There was much animated conversation between Carolyn and Arthur but little other than the ordinary civilities between Margaret and Lawrence.

As the evening progressed, all the men wanted to talk to and dance with Carolyn and Lawrence saw little of her until it was time to depart. He did receive many complimentary remarks about his partner and basked in the reflected glory of her mesmerising presence. When they had mentioned Lawrence she had said of him in her best Texan accent "isn't he a little sweety?"

They walked the short distance home and she enthused about the evening. "You English certainly know how to enjoy yourselves. It's been a perfect evening and very illuminating in meeting all your people and to learn what they think and how they operate," she pronounced. Unknown to Lawrence, it wasn't just the good food, wine and dancing she was referring to. She was a political student and politics and all that it entailed were uppermost in her thoughts. She had learned much that evening. As they were about to part, she thanked him for inviting her and said she would like to see him again next Sunday evening.

He called for her at 7.30 pm and they walked to a restaurant where she had reserved a table. Before they took their place, she suggested an aperitif in the bar area. They sat down in a quiet corner. She had much to say to him and commenced straight away. As soon as the waiter had served the drinks, she turned to him, took his hand and said, "Lawrence, after such a lovely evening last Friday I don't wish to upset you by what I have to say. Please just listen me out and don't be offended because I have your best interests at heart."

"I know," she began "that Headley Carlton-May is to retire in three months time and as his deputy, you will be in pole position to succeed him."

He nodded with some trepidation wondering what she was about to say. He had heard that American girls could be very forceful, outspoken and pushy and in this case, he had heard correctly.

"Lawrence," she began, "there's nothing certain in life and even favourites have to work hard to succeed. Politics can be a nasty business, requiring skill and on occasions a little deviousness. I was, as you know, talking to Arthur Burton at the Civic Ball and he is a very interesting, intelligent and ambitious character. I also watched him closely as he mingled with the mayor and councillors, especially the new ones, introducing himself, shaking their hand and generally making himself known. This is common practice in America and it is obvious to me that he has started his campaign to get the top job. He is a very dangerous rival."

Lawrence looked a little crestfallen and slightly embarrassed, as he knew he had been very much in the background that evening. Perhaps he was relying too much on Headley Carlton-May to promote him and on his current position as deputy in waiting.

He was also beginning to have serious doubts as to whether or not he actually wanted the job. Things had not gone well as of late and the thought of all the extra responsibility was beginning to weigh heavily upon him.

Carolyn saw his face drop. The waiter approached and gave them the menu and after choosing their starter, took their places at the table.

Carolyn continued, "Now is the time to decide if you want this job because if you do there is a lot of catching up and preparation to be done. Would you like me to help you?"

Lawrence looked across at her and nodded appreciatively.

"What do you have in mind?" he asked.

She sat back confidently, knowing that the difficult part of the evening had been overcome. She could now talk to him in a relaxed way and put forward her views and plans.

"Lawrence, getting on in this world is often about what you know and what you say. But equally, its about whom you know, how you say things and how you look. You are an intelligent man with knowledge, experience and ability. We need to harness all these attributes. What I want to do is to meet you early next Saturday morning and we will spend the whole day in the city. It will require some money, so have your credit card ready and regard what you spend as an investment."

She called for him promptly and they walked into the city centre. First stop was a tailor's shop where Lawrence was measured for and tried on several suits. Carolyn made many suggestions and was eventually satisfied with two suits that she described as 'absolutely wonderful'.

"They will need slight adjustment but the manager says that this can be done by Tuesday."

Then they moved across to the casual wear department and an hour later, had purchased a smart sports jacket and two pairs of casual trousers. Ties, shirts and socks were added to the bill. Next on the list were the shoe shops and three pairs purchased. Carolyn had arranged an appointment at an optician for an eye test and purchase of contact lenses. She left him for two hours in the care of two opticians who, after testing his eyesight, taught him how to insert and remove lenses and sold him a month's supply.

"Don't worry if you have a little trouble at first. I wear them myself and you just get used to them," Carolyn had said, adding "and I shall be here to help you."

After a late snack lunch, she took him to the hairdressers, instructing staff on the cut she though he needed. Then it was on to the jewellers where she had seen a watch that she described as 'amazing'. He saw the price and looked shocked, but she insisted that it wasn't any old timepiece but a work of art and would greatly enhance his image.

"I want you to look a billion dollars," she said. "If you look good and feel good, your confidence increases and everything follows from that, believe you me."

When he returned home that evening, he looked at the multitude of receipts and realised he had spent almost the maximum on both his credit cards - about three months salary. He would have to break into his savings for a while and on top of that, he had asked Carolyn to join him at Fielden races on Wednesday afternoon.

By Wednesday, Lawrence had collected his suits and sports clothes and decided to wear the new jacket and pair of casual trousers. He had had a few problems with his contact lenses but was now getting used to them thanks to Carolyn's help. With his new hairstyle he looked a revitalised man. Carolyn as usual wore a dress and hat appropriate for the occasion and both were admired as they walked amongst the race goers. It proved to be a smart decision by Lawrence to attend the races as several council members and influential people in the private sector were present and he was able to introduce Carolyn, speak to them confidently and allow her to tell them how fortunate Fielden City Council was to have such a forward looking deputy chief executive and one who was 'obviously destined for greater things'.

By now, it was generally assumed that as Lawrence was divorced and a free man and Carolyn did not wear an engagement or wedding ring that their relationship was somewhat more than friendly. 'Things are likely to progress', was the considered view around the office.
Carolyn took time out from her studies to socialise with Lawrence and they were regularly seen around town in the shops, bars and restaurants. During this time Lawrence continued to build upon his newly restored self-confidence and was focused on the approaching retirement of Headley Carlton-May. Headley was closely monitoring his work performance and was delighted with Lawrence's improvement. Lawrence had represented the Council at two important enquiries - one on the proposed opening of a new refuse site and the other on outline planning permission to establish out of town shopping. Both proposals had met with significant opposition from residents and small shopkeepers. In each case, Lawrence had shown considerable skill in presenting the Council's case and in demonstrating benefits to sceptical ratepayers. Whilst decisions were still awaited, both the Director of Technical Services and the Chief Planning Officer had warmly praised Lawrence

at Management Team meetings.

In support of her political studies, Carolyn attended several council and committee meetings as an observer in the public gallery. From her vantage point and from contacts with council members, it was clear to her that Lawrence really had impressed, but also that Arthur Burton continued to be highly competent and respected.

A month later, the Council's Human Resources section, on the instruction of Headley Carlton-May, prepared the advertisement for the post of Chief Executive. In accordance with union agreements, the post was advertised among current staff only, with a closing date fourteen days later.

It was the middle of July when the date for applications closed and four applications had been received - from Charles Friend, Director of Technical Services; Kate Prescott, Director of Administration; Arthur Burton and Lawrence Shawcross.

Under the rules, each was entitled to an interview by a sub committee following which a reduced short list of two would be selected to go for interview in the council chamber before all 50 members.

Carolyn ensured that Lawrence looked his best on the occasion of the first interview. Following a nervous morning for all the candidates, the sub committee selected both Lawrence and Arthur. Headley Carlton-May had been present at the interviews and had been pleased with his protégés confident performance. He also recognised that Arthur Burton had performed with great skill too. The two best candidates were going forward but nothing could yet be taken for granted.

A formal letter was sent to both men inviting attendance for interview on 31st July.

When Lawrence showed the letter to Carolyn she gave a sigh of disappointment.

"It's a real pity Lawrence, but our term ends on the 26th and I've already booked a flight home to see family and friends. I'll be back in mid September though."

In the week remaining before Carolyn's departure she talked to him constantly, ensuring that answers to all possible questions were covered. With his self-confidence fully restored and in receipt of a boost from his recent performances at work, he automatically found all the right responses to Carolyn's probing questions. She really was an asset. The word 'asset' proved to be a defining moment in his preparation. Carolyn had said that at some point during the interview, he would be asked to name one quality or asset which would fit him for the post of Chief Executive. "How will you respond to that question?" she had asked. Lawrence thought for some time and replied, "Well, I suppose I am the only candidate with a legal qualification which is a prime requirement for this post."

"That's it!" cried Carolyn. You've hit upon the one thing that Arthur Burton doesn't have, a legal qualification. Sure he could buy expertise in but that would be extra time and cost. Your councillors are demanding people. They want answers immediately. When they ask if a particular course of action is legal, they require an answer there and then. They want a definitive answer not reference back to a later date. Yes, you are the only person with that knowledge and power. Go out there and tell them that."

On the day, the two candidates were interviewed in alphabetical order, each being asked the same questions. Going first, Arthur Burton presented a very persuasive case, answering questions confidently and clearly. In the tense atmosphere of a packed Council chamber, he did once or twice have to wipe the sweat from his brow but he was most impressive, maintaining eye-to-eye contact with the assembled members. In response to 'that' question about his main quality or asset, he stressed his leadership qualities of the Finance Department and referred to the excellent reports it had received from the external auditor. He concluded by thanking members for inviting him for interview.

His was a difficult act to follow and Headley Carlton-May knew that Lawrence would have to display something extra special to sway members.

On entering the Council chamber, Lawrence followed Carolyn's instructions to the letter - 'Stand tall, walk in smartly, sit comfortably, smile confidently, take a little time before answering, then do so in a firm, positive manner'.

His rehearsals with Carolyn had been time well spent. He seemed very much at ease and answered without speaking for too long. He held the members attention and gave knowledgeable responses to all the questions. Yet his replies were not significantly better than Arthur Burton's and it looked to Headley that the decision could go either way.

"Finally Mr Shawcross," asked the Mayor, who was chairing the interview proceedings, "can you tell us what main quality or asset you have that would fit you for this post of Chief Executive?"

Lawrence thought for a few seconds, knowing that this was his big chance. He had rehearsed this with Carolyn and was determined to make his answer pay dividends.

"Mr Mayor," he said slowly, ensuring that he made eye contact with the main body of councillors.

"Mr Mayor, I believe it essential that for this important post a legal background and qualification is vital. You need right and proper advice upon the decisions you will have to take and should any doubt arise, I am qualified to give you such legal opinion without recourse to reference back and delay. That is the asset I possess and that is what you will receive if you choose to appoint me to this post."

Heads nodded around the chamber. Lawrence was thanked by the Mayor and responded by thanking members for the opportunity they had given him.

In the ensuing discussion, members debated the merits of both candidates, finally asking the advice of Headley Carlton-May.

"I think I speak for everyone when I say that this afternoon we have interviewed two excellent candidates, both of whom would fill the post with distinction. I do feel however - and I could see many members agreeing with Mr Shawcross's point - that a legal qualification is vital for the possessor of this post."

That was the clinching statement. The Mayor immediately asked for a show of hands on his proposal that Lawrence Shawcross be appointed. There was only one member, Councillor Mrs Taylor who demurred but hers was a lone voice.

"Then I think I can say the decision is unanimous," concluded the Mayor and Lawrence was called back to the chamber to be offered the post, which he immediately accepted.

After thanking the Mayor and members, Headley Carlton-May invited both Lawrence and the crestfallen Arthur back to his room. Although disappointed, Arthur knew full well that it was no use doing anything other than accept the decision. He congratulated Lawrence and promised his full support.

Lawrence arrived back at his apartment just after 9 pm, elated at the outcome but disappointed that Carolyn was not there to share in his success. He didn't know what he would have done without her. He was already formulating plans for them both in advance of her return in September.

He telephoned his parents to relay the good news and receive their congratulations and answered several calls from his colleagues who all said they were delighted with his appointment.

He had just sat down to relax with a tonic water which was badly needed after all those alcoholic drinks Hartley had poured, when the telephone rang again.

It was Carolyn. She sounded in high spirits, immediately asking how the interview had gone.

"You were so right Carolyn," he enthused, "everything we discussed went as planned and I was offered the job. I can't thank you enough for all you have done."

"Lawrence, I'm so pleased for you," she effused. "You really do deserve it, congratulations, congratulations, congratulations."

She stopped for a second then continued, "You must think I'm a little tipsy and if I am then it's because I'm going to be married, so you must congratulate me my little sweetie."

There was a long pause whilst Lawrence tried to digest what she had said but he remained nonplussed.

"Married?" questioned the baffled Lawrence at last, "married, what do you mean, married? I don't understand."

"Yes, married Lawrence, married. Before I came to England, I had been a friend for several years with Greg but life became a little edgy, uncertain if you know what I mean. So we decided to part for a while to see how things developed. Well, we both now know that we are just right for each other and we will be married at the end of the year. It's been a great day for both of us, so congratulate me my little darling," she giggled.

It sounded down the line that she was definitely the worse for drink, for after hearing her say in a heavy slurred voice "Hey Greg honey, come and talk to my lovely little Lawrence," the phone went dead.

Carolyn never returned to Fielden. A few weeks later, Lawrence saw removal men clearing her apartment and shortly afterwards, new tenants moved in.

Lawrence took up his duties in August. Headley, who had been delighted that his long term strategy of succession planning had once again been proved right, stayed on for a few weeks to help him settle in. Even by the time of his leaving presentation, Headley had already detected a change in Lawrence. Certainly, Lawrence had given a warm, even witty speech and Headley had responded by saying how much he had enjoyed his career at Fielden City Council and how he hoped to stay in touch with his friends. He thanked them profusely for their gift of the complete Ring Cycle of Wagner, which Lawrence had been advised by older officers would be a fitting present in view of his love of all things German.

The change Headley had noticed in Lawrence was his complete refusal to talk about Carolyn. He had remarked to Lawrence that she had been such a beneficial influence on him and asked if he intended to pursue his friendship with her. Lawrence merely said that the friendship, if that is what it had been, had ended and he refused to elaborate. The subject was closed. It followed a similar pattern after his divorce from Hilary and that was not a good sign.

Lawrence did put everything into the job and all the management team, including Arthur Burton, helped him in every possible way. Gradually however, the Lawrence of old began to reappear. The slight hesitancy, lack of attention to detail, draining of self-confidence. One evening, he had a problem with a contact lense. After two hours, he had failed to extract it and next day had to take time off to go to an optician when it was eventually removed. His eye was sore and even worse; he had missed an important meeting. Arthur Burton had taken his place at short notice and dealt so well with the agenda items, that members were reminded just how close he had been to becoming their Chief Executive.

Lawrence threw out the contact lenses and reverted to his thick horned rimmed spectacles. He ignored Carolyn's advice to have a haircut each fortnight so that his hair began to look quite unruly. He started to arrive at the office later than usual and finish as early as possible, delegating many meetings to his subordinates. Members began to query why he was absent so often and why he was not providing the leadership they demanded. Never anything but a fit man, his colleagues were surprised by the number of times he was off work, claiming he was unwell. This state of affairs continued for over a year until one member, frustrated by Lawrence's performance proposed in full Council a 'vote of no confidence in the Chief Executive'. The proposal was not seconded but after the meeting it was clear that many were indeed concerned.

The next Council meeting was scheduled for 10th October but at 6.30 pm Lawrence had failed to arrived. He hadn't sent an apology or contacted any of his colleagues to ask them to stand in. It was therefore proposed that Mr Arthur Burton fulfil the duties of Chief Executive for the meeting. It transpired that Lawrence had been in the office until noon but had left without returning. He had taken papers with him and his secretary had assumed that he must have decided to go straight to the council chamber for the evening meeting.

Later that night, the Director of Technical Services was delegated to find Lawrence to determine the reason for his absence but could obtain no answer at his apartment. The service manager had been called to unlock the door but there was no sign of Lawrence.

Next morning, a cleaner at the Tudor Rose hotel in the City reported at 11.30 am that she could not obtain any response from room No 27 despite knocking many times. The manager was contacted and upon opening the door with a duplicate key, found Lawrence's rigid body prone upon the bed, with the room curtains closed.

He was found later to have taken over one hundred amphetamine tablets the night before.

No note was ever found. It was as though he had made the final decision that was his alone.

His funeral was attended by almost all the staff and council members, but Headley Carlton-May was conspicuous by his absence. Many regrets were expressed at such a tragic early loss of life and Councillor Mrs Taylor was overheard to say to the former Mayor, "All this could have been avoided if only we had gone for A. Burton."

Lord Mayor demands job for Donald

THE TOWN CLERK'S CLERK

Any casual observer catching sight of Donald Partridge scurrying along Trowbury High Street could be forgiven for thinking that there was a circus in town. With a head seemingly far too large for his small, slender frame, a bulbous red nose, bushy eyebrows and shiny bald head, he cut a comical figure of fun guaranteed to make adults laugh and children shout with glee. As he bustled along, this thought was initially underlined by Donald's appearance in his long black jacket and dark striped trousers, both of which were several sizes too large, white shirt, red bow tie and black patent shoes. Hearing him speak in a stuttering, loud, piercing voice, like the sound of a kettle huffing and wheezing as it neared boiling point before eventually emitting a continuous shrill high-pitched whistle, only added confirmation of the onlookers first impression. To the residents who knew him well, Donald Partridge was variously described as bumptious, obnoxious even obscene.

An only child, he had lived in the Cumbrian town all his life and seen it expand from a sleepy coastal resort into a thriving port. He lived with his 93 years old widowed mother at 43, High Street, a large family house acquired by his great grandfather, a sea-faring gentleman, some 150 years ago. At that time in the early Victorian era the town had started to develop with the High Street forming the principal thoroughfare. It was a ribbon development of fine architectural buildings stretching half a mile inland from the shoreline starting at the entry to the port and ending at the Parish Church. Number 43 was mid-point; one of a row of seven splendid detached family houses with large gardens between the Town Hall and Library. After the First World War, all the other houses had gradually ceased to be occupied by families, being sold to property developers for conversion into business premises. Save for a few flats for rent above some of the shops, the Partridge family, or what remained of it, were the street's only permanent residents. Mrs Partridge, having lived there all her life, was both the towns oldest and longest surviving inhabitant. Over the years, the family had reduced in size until, upon Mr Partridge's untimely death at sea some fifty-five years past; Mrs Partridge had been left to bring up the young Donald.

Not for him a life on the high seas in succession to the chosen career of three generations of the Partridge family. Donald had been an awkward child of stunted growth, variously described as difficult and hyper-active which Mrs Partridge had put down to having him late in life. Donald was fortunate in that his mother, in an effort to keep him occupied and harness his abundant energy had regularly taken him to the Library and each Sunday to Church.

The Library was an impressive building of soft sandstone on three floors and square in structure. Many a time, Donald had walked towards it and looked up to read and ponder the words etched into the top eye-line of the building:-

'To Literature, Arts and Science'
' The mental riches you may here acquire abide with you always'

To his mother's disappointment, the delights of literature and the exactness of science had completely eluded Donald. On the subject of Arts however, she had been more than fully compensated by the early talent he had displayed on the piano. His first teacher, a Welshman, was very strict. He used to slam the lid on Donald's fingers if he made a mistake. His mother found a more considerate lady teacher for him. He had an ear for music and she took him up to Grade 8 before announcing that she was going to have twins. That was the end of his formal training.

His first 'professional' engagement at the age of fourteen earned him a large hamper of goods for a five-hour stint playing the piano at a New Years Eve function at a local club. They were so impressed with him that he was retained, playing every Friday and Saturday evenings. Although under age, he picked up a liking for drink and acquired into his vocabulary the entire local bar room language. Mrs Partridge had always played the piano and occasionally the church organ and it was she who introduced Donald to the resident organist and the impressive recently restored 'Henry Wills and Son Ltd' organ. His interest gradually aroused, he derived pleasure in the magic of the organ, but was not a sudden convert. Initially, the number of keyboards, multitude of buttons and pipes and especially the pedal board baffled him. He had to keep looking down for a long time afterwards until he learned to play the pedals properly. His mother encouraged him by purchasing an electronic 'Hammond C3' organ. Although he received good training from the manufacturer, he was literally thrown in at the deep end and managed to pick things up. When the resident church organist retired, Donald was invited to succeed him and he started playing regularly each Sunday morning and evening.

Trying to obtain permanent work for Donald was a different matter altogether. By now, he had a reputation within the local community as an unpredictable, maladjusted individual. He rarely received an invitation to interview from the many applications his mother encouraged him to make. When on the rare occasion he was selected, his appearance, attitude and bad language guaranteed instant rejection. It was only after his mother, a distant relative of the town's Lord Mayor, implored him to use his good offices to find Donald a job with the local council that his career commenced. The Lord Mayor was a persuasive man who talked the Town Clerk into creating a post within his department especially for Donald. As a personal favour to the Lord Mayor, the Town Clerk reluctantly agreed. A sinecure position was devised to cater for Donald's eccentricity but subject to a six month review period. At fifteen years of age, Donald, without any formal qualifications was considered fortunate to have obtained a position that might offer secure employment and an opportunity for advancement although he was not expected to be retained at the end of his trial period, if indeed he ever reached it.

During that era, employment was plentiful and assessment not over rigorous. The Lord Mayor, pleased to see that Donald had followed his mothers advice never to be absent from work, made quite sure that his appointment became permanent.

As junior clerk, he was retained but never promoted being more errand boy than office boy. Told to make tea and distribute post, his few clerical duties were subject to strict supervision. For a quarter of a century he had served three previous Town Clerk's to the best of his limited ability. Several times applying for promotion he had been overlooked and remained on the lowest clerical salary scale.

The present Town Clerk of twenty years, Godfrey Hunter had been appointed to bring a more business-like approach to proceedings and develop the town as befitted its growing status and financial importance. After first observing Donald's odd appearance, then hearing his stuttering high-pitched outpourings, he ventured to ask his colleagues "who is that bumptious little clown?"

He had been horrified to be told that he was a member of his staff and determined to change him. He was soon to realise that although Donald was offensively conceited with occasional outbursts of cursing and swearing, he was very much set in his ways.

Times and customs had radically altered during Donald's twenty-five years service with the Town Council but he had not moved with them. Nor was he disposed to. His dress sense derived from following his mother's advice to always look the part of a Town Hall clerk. To her mind, that resembled something from a Dickensian novel. She insisted that he order six pairs of each type of clothes to last him a lifetime. The showman in him had cultivated his somewhat eccentric style and he saw no reason to change.

Despite Donald having an inflated opinion of his importance, Godfrey Hunter warmed to his plain speaking, no nonsense bustling style and found him to be totally loyal. He accepted Donald's quirks and occasional gaffs with understanding. No more so than when Donald was asked to stand at the door and vet members of the public wishing to be allowed entry to listen to an important debate. Upon seeing a reporter who had recently maligned his Town Clerk in a recent press article, Donald had rushed over to him, grabbed his arm and blurted out in his loud voice that everyone could hear, "an, an, y, you c ,c, can f, f, fuck off for a s, s, start."

With one protector at work, Donald also had another during his leisure. Previous vicars had merely tolerated his presence as organist on Sunday's. Both administration and congregation disliked his obnoxious manner. Totally immersed in his playing, he was oblivious of instructions. Frequently, when the vicar had announced that the congregation would sing just the first two and last verse of a particular hymn, to the consternation of all, Donald would continue on, playing every verse. A further irritation was his habit of improvisation and playing to the full power of the organ. This not only confused the choir but also obliterated their singing even when at full compliment.

Following his early experience of pub music, Donald cultivated an impressive classical repertoire ranging from Albinoni to Wagner, performing Saturday morning recitals and at the occasional wedding or funeral service. He always played a combination of church music written for the organ and a selection of classical works. When asked to play *I did it my way* at a funeral, he rounded on the bereaved informing them, "Th, th, this is T, Trowbury not b, b, bloody Glastonbury!"
The present vicar, Reverend Shelsdon, displayed a more liberal view towards Donald because he respected his playing and was well aware that after twenty-five years of Donald at the helm, reliable organists had become scarce and a competent replacement well nigh impossible to find. Donald's mother had drummed into him that playing for the church was a vocation and he had always given his services freely.

Donald's life could never have been described as exciting. To the outsider, it seemed completely devoid of variety. He was a true home town boy, having travelled little, liking the security and comfort of his known environment. He had only once been to London, describing it as 'a little bit off the beaten track, stuck in the south-east corner of England'.
43, High Street was far too big for just Donald and his mother but she flatly refused to consider moving. Having been born in the house and lived there all her life, she was determined to die there. Five of the six upstairs bedrooms had been unoccupied for many years. Donald could only just remember going into them as a child. Since the deaths of his grandparents and father, his mother had arranged for the doors to be securely locked and Donald had no idea of the key's whereabouts.
He had use of the remaining bedroom and bathroom. As time passed, his mother's reduced mobility had necessitated internal ground floor adaptations. Now, she occupied a spacious former study area converted into an en-suite bedroom. They shared the kitchen, lounge and dining room and Donald had exclusive use of the library room which housed his electric Hammond organ and a piano. After household chores, he spent most evenings in this room playing his favourite music and consuming his only luxury, an extensive stock of malt whisky.
In recent years, Social Services had granted Mrs Partridge an attendance allowance from which she managed to engage a part-time cleaner and

she received meals-on-wheels each day. Apart from that, Donald was occupied in looking after her and managing household bills. Between them they shared expenses. Although money was scarce on Donald's meagre earnings and his mother's state pension, they just about managed. Their large garden contained a small orchard that produced cherries, apples and pears in season that Donald collected and sold to the greengrocer. It was a help but that was about all. The family car had long since gone. Donald had never driven and ever since his mother had given up her licence, they had had to rely upon public transport or simply walk. The cleaner regularly provided Donald with a list of shopping requirements that he purchased in dribs and drabs each week after several visits on foot to the discount stores.

Donald was in the habit of returning home for lunch but occasionally was requested to man the office when the receptionist required time off. One of Donald's few onerous duties was to raise and dispatch sundry debtor accounts to residents who had entered into an agreement with the Town Council. Several such contracts concerned lease of land for agricultural or recreational purposes. Donald knew all the farmers, horse owners and sporting club secretaries by name and his task had become second-nature after all his years of experience. He merely checked the minutes for the agreed charge, wrote out the account, which was double checked by the Town Clerk's secretary and posted it. The accounts were to be paid to the Town Treasurer at his cash office across the road. Donald was informed when the sums had been settled and stamped copy accounts as 'PAID'.

One lunchtime when Donald was on stand-by duty in the Town Clerk's office, local farmer Dan Compton entered, intent on paying his annual licence fee.

"Donald," he exclaimed, "You put the fear of God into those bats in the church rafters last Sunday morning, not to mention all the congregation. Bit excessive on the bass notes and peddle if you don't mind me saying so. The sound reverberated throughout the church and didn't do my ears much good either."

"You, you, you can't soft p, p, peddle with p, p, powerful church music," retorted Donald. "Tha, tha, that's how it was w, w, written and th, tha, that's how I p, p, play it."

Dan quickly changed the subject."How's that old mother of yours keeping? She must be a good age now."

"R, r, reached 93 last month a, a, and going f, f, fine," replied Donald. They spoke for several minutes before Dan Compton looked up at the clock.

"Good God, can't spend all my time talking. I've got work to do, animals to feed and a wife and kids to provide for. I've just come to pay my bill."

"Wr, wr, wrong office." replied Donald. "T, T, Treasurer's office is across r, r, road."

"No time Donald," said Dan, taking a large sealed envelope from his pocket and thrusting it into Donald's hand. "Do me a favour and take it across for me."

Six months later, after sending out a reminder, the Treasurer's cash office received a personal call from an angry Dan Compton.

"What the hell's all this about?" he demanded, pushing the reminder letter into the cashiers hand. "I paid this months ago."

The cashier checked the computer records. "No sir, it shows here as outstanding!"

"Bloody computers! You haven't recorded it properly, that's for sure," responded an indignant Dan Compton.

"Sorry sir, it shows here as unpaid. Where is your receipt?" asked the cashier.

"Receipt? Don't be silly, I've known Donald Partridge for years. I gave him the money to pay in for me and that's a fact," Dan shouted back.

The Town Clerk was told and immediately demanded that Donald come to his office. Donald entered, taking his usual short hurried steps to the offered seat across from the Town Clerk's desk.

"Donald, what did you do with Dan Compton's money?" asked the Town Clerk gently.

Donald's usual self-assertiveness evaporated. He opened his mouth to speak but this time the kettle was well below boiling point and no words came forth. He wriggled uncomfortably in his seat, wrung his hands nervously and appeared at a loss for words. At long last, the kettle's boiling point arrived and he blurted out, "He, he, he gave me this envelope. I, I, I know I should have p, p, paid it in but the b, b, big house is expensive to r, r, run and r, r, repairs had to be done. M, M, Mother gives me money from her p, p, pension but even with my s, s, small s, s, salary it is hardly enough to make ends meet. Sh, Sh, She won't move. It's her home and I, I, I have no alternative but to s, s, stay and l, l, look after her. P, p, problems are always arising with the old house and I, I, I had to p, p, pay an expensive bill to r, r, repair old g, g, guttering. When, when, when Dan Compton gave me t, t, that envelope, I op, op, opened it and *had never seen so much money in all my life.* I, I, I was t, t, tempted. I, I, I've never been dishonest before and it will k, k, kill my mother if she ever f, f, finds out. "I, I, I'll pay it off if I, I, I can in s, s, stages but p, p, please don't s, s, say anything," he pleaded. "All right Donald. Go back to your desk. Your position and secret are safe with me," said Godfrey Hunter kindly.

Later that afternoon Godfrey Hunter contacted the Treasurer and instructed him to cancel the reminder.

The Treasurer regarded him knowingly. "He'll have to go Godfrey," he said.

Godfrey Hunter, in deep thought, seemed to nod in agreement. Then, speaking slowly, he addressed the Treasurer directly. "Yes, normally, there would be no question about it, but the money has now be fully repaid. Donald told me that if his mother found out it would kill her, but it's Donald I am most concerned about. I think that if the news got out it would be Donald who would be most affected and I regard him as a possible suicide case. I know that he can be objectionable and abusive but he hasn't had much out of life. He has looked after his mother for so long that any change to his routine and finances could affect his mind. He has been loyally in post for over forty-five years and I am going to recommend to Town Council that he retire next year on full pension when he becomes sixty. That way, there will be no stain on his character."

In the event and feeling a little sorry for Donald' circumstances, the Town Clerk exercised his discretion to grant him two additional salary increments. Officially, it was nothing to do with the fact that the Town Clerk knew his salary and perks to be ten times greater than Donald's nor that it was a means of increasing Donald's lump sum payment and pension for the rest of his life. It was stated to be in recognition of his loyal and dedicated service throughout his career.

The following year, Donald retired on a relatively small but full pension. He continued to look after his mother, to play his music both at home and in church and enjoy a drink or two in his library each evening. The household bills became even harder to meet and it was only Donald's lump sum retirement payment that enabled them to pay their way without recourse to debt.

In the end, Mrs Partridge's wish was realised when, aged ninety-six she passed away peacefully in the house where she had been born.

Donald was unable to cope with such a large property and began looking for a small flat in the High Street where he could live within his means and continue his life in town. Shortly, he instructed agents to place 43, High Street on the market but not before executors had also completed the assessment of the value of its land and contents. Keys could not be found for the locks to the five unused bedrooms and it was necessary to force the doors. Each room had been in total darkness throughout the years with thick curtains pulled across the windows and dust covers placed over the furniture and other contents. Numerous trunks and artefacts from Donald's great-grandfather, grandfather and father's travels were revealed.

It was a veritable Aladdin's cave. The executors unearthed silk materials from Persia and China including quality hand made silk goods fashioned into ladies clothes, bedspreads, pillowcases and tablecloths. Best of all, there were well preserved rugs and carpets with intricate ornate patterns, some for wall hanging as tapestries. From the Orient, Spain, Italy, France, Germany, America, Africa, and Russia came books and manuscripts; porcelain, gold, silverware and platinum; jewellery and gemstones of amber, emerald, jade, sapphire, ruby and ivory; and a collection of paintings - sketches and drawings in oils, watercolours, graphite and inks. There were over two thousand items ranging from ornamental silver plates, coins, cutlery, clasps, buckles, amulets, ear-rings, bangles, necklaces, rings, crosses, brooches, down to the smallest tie-pin.

A London firm specialising in fine arts was contacted. They transported the treasure trove to their saleroom where, behind the scenes, they were carefully examined, cleaned, valued, catalogued and auctioned. Following sale of the house and grounds, all of Donald's mother's assets had been disposed of.

A copy of the local morning paper was always in the post for both the Town Clerk and Treasurer. It wasn't long before they were speaking on the telephone about the front-page headline referring to Mrs Molly Partridge.

'LOCAL WOMAN LEAVES FORTUNE'

The last Will and Testament of Mrs Molly Partridge late of 43, High Street, Trowbury realised £4,628,569 gross. Except for two bequests of £5,000 to the local church organ fund and the library, the remainder goes to the sole beneficiary, her son, Mr Donald Partridge.

Town Clerk Godfrey Hunter recalled Donald's statement about Dan Compton's lease of land payment - *"I had never seen so much money in all my life."*
And Donald and his mother had been scraping a living throughout their lives, surrounded by this vast amount of wealth.
Godfrey Hunter, deep in thought, smiled ruefully to himself. Donald has become a rich man and good luck to him. The Chancellor of the Exchequer will receive his Inheritance Tax in due course but I don't suppose I shall ever see my money back.

AMATEUR DRAMATICS

Half an hour before the curtain was due to go up on the year-end production of Trenton Friars Amateur Dramatic Society, the bulky figure of Sean O'Day pushed opened his front door to calls of 'good luck' from his wife and children. Stepping out, he pulled the door firmly shut and started the two minutes walk towards the village hall. The evening would mark his stage debut but he displayed no sign of stage fright. He was well rehearsed, knew that the cast had confidence in his ability and that he would not let them down. His was an undemanding role but a vital one requiring total concentration.

The audience packed into the small village hall anticipated an evening of excitement, suspense and mystery. The year's two other productions (performed on Friday evening with a Saturday afternoon matinee) had not been well supported. A Christmas special, vaguely based on a Dickensian theme and an Easter extravaganza aimed at children somewhat reminiscent of Roald Dahl's 'Charlie and the Chocolate Factory' had not been the expected sell-outs, resulting in heavy losses for the Society. Received wisdom was that the ticket price had been far too high.

The final summer presentation on Saturday evening was entirely different - a murder mystery - following which the audience were to be invited to vote for the outstanding performer. And, entrance was free of charge with complimentary tea and biscuits during the interval!

Director and amateur playwright Philip Goodhurste had written the play and considered it to be his *magnum opus*, unsurpassed in plot, dialogue and outcome by any of the world's past or present eminent authors of the genre. A sure fire hit that would take the theatre world by storm, be embraced by famous companies and like 'The Mousetrap,' run and run and run. All that was required to achieve this sublime outcome was first class direction, a competent well-rehearsed cast and critical acclaim. Philip, having written the material was also an experienced amateur director with many past successes to his credit. As art critic for the local and regional press under the pseudonym 'In the Box Seat' he would have no difficulty in informing the art world of the achievement of theatrical entertainment previously thought unattainable.

And yet, he was not entirely comfortable with the way things had developed. The enthusiastic cast were the usual mixture of hopefuls and has-beens. At least they were committed and under Philip's sympathetic direction always gave of their best, occasionally displaying hitherto unknown talents to the delight of their relatives and friends in the audience.

Philip's real worry was a newcomer to the society, local businessman Clive Forstone. A pushy individual, he liked to remind people that he was a self-made man who had risen from humble beginnings to his present influential status. Immediately upon joining and being introduced to Philip, he had wasted no time in telling him of his unrivalled ability to mesmerise an audience. By dint of his forceful personality and bulging bank balance he coerced the society's treasurer into recommending to Philip that, in recognition of underwriting the societies debts and provision of free seats at the next production, he would be chosen to play the leading man. In the interests of keeping the society afloat, Philip had reluctantly agreed and given Clive Forstone a copy of the script and the role of investigating Inspector. Philip had been flattered and pleasantly surprised when at first rehearsal, Clive had not only praised his writing skills but had displayed more than a little acting talent.

Clive Forstone had also proposed the audience vote for the outstanding performer, having no doubt as to the outcome and subsequent prestige it would confer upon him.

To add further lustre to the occasion, he had persuaded the mayor of the local Town Council, one Dorothy-Jane Woodfull, to attend and be available on stage to present the coveted award at the end of the evening.

Clive subsequently missed several rehearsals but remained in regular contact, informing Philip that despite his heavy workload he had read the complete script in detail and mastered every twist and turn of the plot. Used to public speaking, he was also adept at improvisation and was certain there would be nothing to worry about.

If Philip had misgivings about Clive himself, he also had concerns about the effect this brash individual might have on the performance of the rest of the cast. But it was too late to change now. Philip consoled himself with the thought that it being **his** play under **his** direction, he might be reading too much into things. All but two of the cast, Sean O'Day and

Clive Forstone had worked with him successfully in the past but still niggling in the back of his mind was the wanton disclaimer used by investment companies that 'past results are no guarantee of future performance and you could lose some or all of your money'.

Sean O'Day arrived a few minutes before the hall lights were extinguished and the audience had settled down in hushed anticipation. He had no need of last minute coaching and had taken his place on stage immediately in advance of the slow, deliberate rise of the curtain.

For a few seconds the audience was greeted by a stage in total darkness until at the click of a switch, a light revealed a cleaning lady in a long white overall entering a library. Around the walls were floor to ceiling bookcases containing hundreds of leather bound volumes. Desks, tables and chairs were scattered randomly throughout the room together with a three-piece suite. There were various ornaments on the tables and a grandfather clock ticking away in one corner. The cleaner was seen making her way towards a large fireplace embedded in the far wall.

She started to clean the grate and prepare to make a warming fire for the day. After some considerable time she turned, then jumped up in the air emitting a piercing shriek that made the audience fall about laughing. The object of her alarm was the sight of the large frame of a man, lying on his side in a pool of red liquid, his back to the audience. A long, leather handled steel dagger clearly protruded from his body.

This was the form of Sean O'Day making his acting debut. As soon as the stage had been illuminated his huddled form was the first thing the audience had seen. The cause of their unconfined mirth was the fact that it had taken the cleaner - Myra Hobday from the high street art shop - an eternity to discover it. Myra Hobday wasn't known to play down her acting skills. With the whole stage at her disposal and an eye on the coveted best performer prize, she began swinging her arms, jumping and leaping around like a whirling dervish, shouting and screaming "murder, murder, call the police, call an ambulance."

She yelled for the bellboy and eventually a young man appeared dressed in pyjama's having evidently just got out of bed. This further amused the audience as whoever was in charge of stage management hadn't noticed that the grandfather clock was showing the time to be twenty past two. A further delay occurred when the bellboy was sent to raise the mistress of the house during which time, Myra Hobday scurried continuously around the library, wringing her hands in anguish, crying "he's dead, look at all that blood."

The body of Sean O'Day remained motionless.

In her own good time, the mistress, Lady Velma Fernyhough duly appeared prompting more histrionics from Myra Hobday. Kneeling down next to the body as if to confirm that it really was lifeless, she then stood up to find the front of her white overall covered in bright red paint. (more laughter).

Lady Velma at last walked across to the telephone prominently placed on a table next to the door, pulled up a nearby chair, sat down and called the police.

"Oh, if only I'd seen the phone I would have called them myself," screamed an ever more animated Myra Hobday, to further uncontrolled mirth.

Hardly had the laughter died down when it started again as within a few seconds of Lady Velma's call the tall figure of Clive Forstone, wearing a deerstalker hat appeared at the door with the words, "I got your call and came as quickly as I could. I've contacted the pathology unit who are on their way."

Entering the room oblivious to the substantial figure of Sean O'Day immediately in front of him, he demanded incredulously, "Where's the body?"

Rising imperiously from her chair, Lady Velma pointed to the unmoving form of Sean O'Day, declaring in her deep, booming voice, "It's there. I think he's been stabbed." (loud laughter).

Clive Forstone now attempted to take control. "As Inspector, I shall be the judge of that. Things are not always as they appear." (more uncontrolled merriment).

The bellboy, who had returned to the stage in his working clothes just in time to hear this statement involuntarily blurted out "that's pretty obvious Mister innit wive that big dagger sticking out of 'is side," and moved towards the body (audience now in a state of euphoria).

"Keep back," admonished the Inspector, annoyed that the young man had been the first to ad lib, a preserve he considered to be his particular speciality. It caused him to advance the script by several lines. "Nothing must be touched until the pathologist has examined the corpse."

At that point, the pathologist and his team should have entered the room but the bellboy's deviation from the script had thrown everything into disarray and they were totally unprepared.

Realising that nothing was happening, the Inspector raised his voice. "I think I hear the pathologist."

Lady Velma crossed to the door and opened it but no one was to be seen. Through clenched teeth, the Inspector muttered "where the hell are they?" a phrase picked up by the on-stage microphones. Through more peals of laughter, he sought to regain his poise, strode through the door with the words "leave this to me, I'll go and find them."

Backstage, the unfortunate pathologist was grabbed by his suit lapels and projected through the door onto the stage by the determined Inspector. Two assistants carrying a stretcher meekly followed.

"Nothing we can do until you've given us the all clear," grunted the exasperated Inspector pointing to the corpse, "but be quick about it, we haven't got all day."

By entering the stage in undue haste, the pathologist had inadvertently left his case outside. He scurried to retrieve it leaving the rest of the cast in limbo. The Inspector, who was still cursing under his breath, busied himself by taking photographs of the scene of crime and Myra Hobday again started to whirl distraughtly around the stage.

When the pathologist appeared carrying his large leather case (to encouraging applause from the audience), he bent down and started to prod the body and study the immediate area. Taking plastic bags from his case, he placed samples into them for further examination. He then told his assistants that they might now remove the body.

Being a big man it was a difficult task for just two men to lift Sean O'Day onto the stretcher. It took the additional help of the pathologist and Inspector to carry him off-stage to appreciative applause and more gales of laughter when 'the dead body' raised an arm in acknowledgement.

Philip Goodhurste had been following developments with growing horror. What was supposed to be a tense, gripping drama had descended into a farcical tragi-comedy. As the corpse was carried off stage he ordered the curtain to be dropped even though it was not the end of the first act. The production had been, in his eyes, shambolic and there was still the second half to follow! Seizing the public microphone, he announced that tea and biscuits would now be served.

During the interval, the cast received feedback that the audience had thoroughly enjoyed the abbreviated first act and had rarely laughed so much in all their lives.
Sean O'Day, stiff after lying on an unyielding stage floor for thirty minutes was in need of exercise. His role successfully accomplished, he decided to walk straight back home and have an early night.

His wife asked him how things had gone.
"I'm not sure," was his puzzled reply. "It was supposed to be a serious drama, I mean, murder is no joking matter, but the audience were laughing all through the first act and gave us a good round of applause when they carried me off stage. Then, unexpectedly, everyone followed and the curtain came down. I didn't know what was going on but my part in the play was over, so I took a much needed walk home."
"Well, as long as you enjoyed the role," said his wife.
"Yes, I did enjoy it, but I don't think lying on the floor for half an hour will lead to an acting career."

An hour and a half later, as he was about to retire to bed, the telephone rang. It was Tom, Sean's next-door neighbour, who had been in the audience, calling to tell him the good news.
"Sean, you've won the best performer award. The Mayor in her full regalia is waiting on stage to present the prize to you with the photographers and press in attendance, so you'd better get back down here straight away."
A bemused Sean dashed back to the village hall. There was no sign of Philip Goodhurste, Clive Forston or Myra Hobday but Mayor Dorothy-Jane Woodfull was waiting together with the rest of the cast and most of the audience.
A smiling Mayor shook his hand warmly, congratulated him upon his success and thrust into his hand the best performance prize, a gold plated statuette. As photographs were being taken of the event, Sean received his

second ovation of the evening. In response, all he could think of to say to the press was that like his role in the play, he was totally speechless.

Back home, Tom explained to Sean and his wife that everyone thought the second half to be even funnier than the first.
"That Inspector chap, who was obviously under-rehearsed, kept bungling his lines and confusing the rest of the cast by ad libbing. The cleaner did her best to up-stage everyone by acting like a windmill in perpetual motion and the rest of the players gave chaotic performances. You should have seen their faces, especially that of the Inspector when it was announced that you had won the award. But we unanimously thought you deserved it.

After Tom had left, Sean's wife congratulated him upon his success.
"It's a right turn-up for the books," he mused, admiring his statuette as proudly as any famous Hollywood actor. "The funny thing is that I didn't stay on long enough to find out who murdered me."

Next day, both local and regional newspapers carried prominently displayed pictures of Sean receiving his 'Oscar' from the Mayor under the heading 'Dead man rises to the occasion' but reluctantly had to inform readers that, 'due to the unfortunate indisposition of our correspondent, 'In the Box Seat' has had to be held over until next week'.
It never appeared.

OBSESSION

As Gael Andreakos drove the short distance from her smart detached house toward her friend Laura's flat in the port of Eastingleigh, her usual smiling, happy go lucky demeanour had given way to a thoughtful, serious expression. Not yet nineteen years of age, life had recently been good to Gael but for the first time she could sense that she was threatened and not fully in control.

She had just been dismissed her from her job following undue pressure and harassment by her manager, Mr Paul Gerrard.

Gael's husband was working abroad and she needed advice. The straight talking Laura was the first person she thought of.

Laura Gifford was two years older than Gael. They had grown up on the same small council housing estate where facilities were few, unemployment high and petty crime an accepted part of day-to-day living. For young school leavers without qualifications, especially girls such as Laura and Gael, job prospects were slim. Whilst the port was busy with a large fishing fleet and a deep water harbour for import/export of fuel and building materials, the town itself was grubby, having seen better days. The two girls however possessed one priceless asset. Both were attractive to men. Knowing of this, they purposely dressed to attract them and enjoyed the attention men afforded them.

Laura, a slim, long haired redhead was an only child of a divorced uncaring mother. After the divorce, the mother had brought home a succession of 'men-friends' and Laura had been left to fend for herself. Eventually, her mother became engaged and moved to live permanently with her boyfriend at his house on the other side of town.

Laura had, like her mother before her, graduated from a girl looking for work during the day to patrolling the dockside for custom in the early evenings. Now, with her good looks, she soon established a regular clientele with business enhanced by the availability of the flat instead of cheap dockside hotel rooms. Her mother, whilst not necessarily approving of her daughter's occupation nevertheless advised her to take all necessary precautions. Whatever steps she did take proved to be ineffective as just before her eighteenth birthday, she gave birth to a baby boy. Her activities and income temporarily curtailed, she resolved to recommence as soon as her figure was back in trim.

Gael in the meantime had left school and like Laura before her was unable to find employment. She advertised her services as a baby sitter, keen to be out of her home environment.

An only child of just four years of age when her father had died, her mother had soon remarried and produced three further children to a feckless husband who was more out of work than in. There was always arguing, noise and tension within the household with continual shouting and fighting between the younger children. Her mother did her best to cope and Gael had tried her utmost to reconcile differences but it had been a thankless task. Now, Gael had developed ambitions far beyond the mundane poverty level of her childhood.

When Laura read Gael's advertisement, she contacted her and it was agreed that Gael would be employed as baby-minder to enable Laura to resume her business.

Gael was a tall, graceful blond-haired, blue-eyed girl with a cheerful smile and an attractive line in conversation. She had had a stream of boyfriends, avidly searching the charity clothes shops in an effort to dress attractively for them but at just sixteen, she was still quite naïve and short of ready money.

With the experience of younger siblings, she was well aware of the demands made by a new baby and at once coped admirably with them. She did take a little time to understand the operation of Laura's business but, acting also as doorkeeper to the numerous men who called at the flat in the early evening, she gradually became accustomed to the system. She arranged to look after the baby in the kitchen so that the lounge was free for customers to await Laura's availability. Gael was the intermediary, offering the 'gentlemen', as Laura called them, a beer or soft drink and making small talk until Laura was ready to take them to the bedroom. Gael was on duty from 6 pm until 10 pm and paid what she considered to be a generous sum.

One day, after several months of this working arrangement, Gael arrived to find Laura snuffling and sneezing, croaking that she was suffering from a bout of flu.

"You could do me a favour and make yourself a bit of pin money," suggested Laura in a hoarse whisper.

"I only have two clients booked for this evening. You know them, the two young trawler men who came yesterday. It's their last evening before they leave tomorrow for another three weeks fishing trip and they always have plenty of ready money to spend. They've both told me what an attractive assistant I have, so how about standing in for me this evening?"

Laura had developed into an uncompromising, hard-headed businesswoman, adept at manipulating others and getting her own way. Faced with her forceful, demanding personality and feeling sorry for her friend, Gael somewhat reluctantly acquiesced. The two young men required little encouragement. Before they went to the bedroom she had asked them, as Laura had told her to, for the 'usual rate' and they had immediately thrust £100 into her hand.

'So this is pin money', thought Gael. The men seemed pleased with her, treated her considerately and she was surprised to find the experience far less onerous than she had imagined. And all that money for something that she had enjoyed and that had not lasted very long!

After that initiation, with Laura's approval, Gael established a small regular clientele of her own. One such person was an older man who arrived in the early evening without prior arrangement. Laura was busy and Gael engaged him in conversation until Laura appeared. Laura took one look at him and said abruptly that business had closed for the evening and that 'perhaps something could be arranged for the future'. Afterwards Laura said that he was too old her liking.

The following week, the man returned. Gael took him into the kitchen and he seemed more than content to remain in her company, drink some beer and talk to her whilst she attended to the baby's needs. After an hour he left having made no demands, paying for his beer and giving her a generous tip.

His visits became a weekly event. To Gael, he was initially like the father she would have liked but never had. Now in his early fifties, he came across as affable but obviously lonely.

Little by little he told Gael details of his life. Married for thirty years, his wife was mainly content to remain at home in the evenings to watch television or read. Her only friend was a neighbour, Patrick Harper, a coal merchant who lived alone in a house fifty yards down the road. They visited each other from time to time ostensibly for her to help him with his business paperwork. He had once confronted Patrick Harper about their relationship but had been menaced and backed down when faced by this rough-hewn individual. There was obviously no love lost between them and they had never since spoken.

The lifestyles of him and his wife were incompatible but she being a staunch Catholic and regular churchgoer would never agree to a divorce. Although under the same roof, they lived separate lives. He was the earner, paying all bills without question in return for a life with few marital obligations and considerable freedom. He still retained an intense dislike of Patrick Harper and despised his wife's refusal to divorce him. Always one to enjoy an active social life he liked nothing better than an evening out at a restaurant or club. His acquired liking for drink was obvious from his bulbous red nose and overweight, somewhat flabby appearance. This he tried to conceal by dressing smartly and he presented himself in such a courteous manner that people took to him at once. Gael was no exception. Impressed by his educated upbringing, witty informal conversation and considerate manner, she found herself attracted to him.

This was Paul Gerrard, once a promising young man with administrative talent who by sheer ability had obtained a law degree, eventually becoming deputy chief executive of the local council. At one time, he was destined to succeed the outgoing chief executive but his unhappy marriage and drinking habits had turned councillors against him.

One councillor in particular who felt contempt for him was Walter Spedding. As Deputy Mayor of the Borough, he had stood-in for the Mayor one afternoon at the customary drinks invitation to departmental staff to celebrate the festive season. In the Chief Executive's absence, Paul Gerrard had had the task of responding to the Deputy Mayor's best wishes for Christmas and New Year. By this time, having consumed a number of alcoholic drinks in addition to his regular lunchtime tipple, his delivery was hesitant and slurred. He attempted to make several risqué jokes that were inappropriate and not well received by the embarrassed staff. Walter Spedding had to eventually step in to, as he later reported to the Chief Executive, 'save him from further punishment'. Councillor Spedding was convinced that Paul Gerrard was not a fit and suitable person to be employed by the council. If he could not be dismissed then he must be given all encouragement to seek a post elsewhere.

Following that Christmas debacle, Paul Gerrard had retained his job by the skin of his teeth but by-passed for the top post when the present Chief Executive had himself obtained a position with another authority.

Various people had tried to help Paul Gerrard but he was always adamant that although a social drinker it did not affect his judgement. He rejected any reference to his being an alcoholic. Such people he had maintained drank throughout the day, had financial problems, slept rough out in the open air and were unemployable. He was none of those. A liking for drink yes, but not a dependency upon it!

Initially, all this was unknown to Gael as they talked. When Paul Gerrard became aware of her desire for self-improvement, it was he who suggested that she might apply for the vacant post of receptionist/telephonist with the council. What he didn't tell her was that he would be interviewing for the post and would have the final say in the appointment process.

Gael leapt at the chance of a daytime job that would get her out of her disruptive home environment and provide her with welcome additional income. She was interviewed in the presence of Mr Paul Gerrard and duly appointed.

She started at once and immediately, her attractive appearance, manner of dealing with people and cheerful disposition impressed everyone from the general clerical staff upwards to the new Chief Executive. He congratulated his deputy on his choice of staff and for a while, Paul Gerrards' reputation rose in the eyes of his colleagues.

It was not to last.

Gael continued with her small clientele in the evenings at Laura's flat and Paul Gerrard continued to visit at least once a week. In due course, he also became a regular customer of Gael and paid her well for the privilege. Flattered by Gael's attention to him and her uplifting presence in his life, he became totally obsessed with her. So much so that he increased his visits to a least twice a week and bought her expensive presents.

This situation continued for several months but was abruptly brought to a halt by the plight of Laura's mother. Her engagement had proved to be far from the romantic prelude to marriage and following a succession of scenes and angry exchanges, she had been summarily ejected from the house of her boyfriend. With the relationship at an end, she had no alternative but to return to live in her flat.

Gael had to inform Paul Gerrard that her services were no longer available to him.Unable to accept the situation, nor indeed wanting to conclude their arrangement, he was instrumental in suggesting that Laura, as a single parent would be regarded as a high priority case in allocation of available council accommodation. He gave Gael the necessary forms for Laura to complete and within a month, she had been allocated a ground floor council flat in a new apartment block.

Suitable accommodation restored, Laura and Gael combined again to provide and please their clients with their services. They were at pains to ensure that the flat was always clean and tidy, and noise kept to a minimum so as not to inconvenience neighbours or draw undue attention to their activities that were strictly outside the terms of the tenancy agreement.

The girl's reputations grew to the point that new customers were neither sought nor encouraged. One exception was a very insistent Greek gentleman, Sampson Andreakos who persisted in randomly calling at the flat. Several times within the same week he would call, followed by a gap of several weeks before his next visits. Like Paul Gerrard, Sampson Andreakos was somewhat older than Laura's regular customers and it was Gael who always attended to him. He made no demands and was content to have a glass of wine and talk.

He was different from the rest, not pushy, brash, boastful or flaunting his money, but a sincere gentleman. Gael found him easy to talk with and soon established that he was captain of a Greek cargo tanker transporting fuel from Eastingleigh port refinery to destinations throughout Europe. In his forties and unmarried, he had spent his life at sea on a rota of fuel transportation to various ports followed by four or five days shore leave. He had heard about the beautiful, vivacious blond girl called Gael from his colleagues and wished to meet her to judge for himself. He had not been disappointed. Once he had met her, he was smitten.

He was looking forward to retirement at fifty and a relaxing life back in his home village on the Island of Pirimos. He had already built a house there. With money saved towards a comfortable future, he was seeking someone to share it with. He could have had the pick of any number of eligible women in his homeland or indeed in any of the ports he frequented but it was Gael with whom he had quickly became infatuated. He didn't ask to become one of her customers but during his short time in port, called for her at the office and took her out at lunchtimes. Gael found him attractive with his Mediterranean appearance and slow, heavily accented English speech and began to miss him when he was away. She was delighted when he sent her postcards and letters from what seemed to her to be such romantic European destinations.

Her evenings at Laura's flat continued with the usual callers including the now more than ever demanding Paul Gerrard. His attitude towards her had changed and she began to feel that he regarded her as his possession; a sort of reward for the favours he had done in obtaining a job for her and the flat for Laura.

And yet, whilst she still acknowledged gratitude for his actions and recognised his support for her, she had begun to regard his rewards as benefiting Laura more than herself, feeling that he was just using her. She had to be adroit in making herself available for him without the conflict of others demanding her attention. She now knew that this sort of life was not for her, just a means to an end in helping achieve her ambition of a happy, secure and successful future.

She looked forward to Sampson Andreakos's visits. He was an honest, clever and astute man. Gael found herself thinking more and more about him, of his background, his country and his lifestyle. It seemed far removed from her humble, troubled upbringing and her humdrum home life.

Gael was disappointed on the morning of her eighteenth birthday that she had not heard from Sampson for several days. Just before lunchtime, a taxi drew up outside the offices and she was overjoyed to see Sampson walk into the reception area carrying a large bouquet. Over lunch, he presented her with an expensive diamond engagement ring. She did not have to think twice about accepting. She was of an age to decide upon her own future. Marriage to the seemingly wealthy Sampson was her passport to prosperity, to a future she had but dreamt of. It also had the further advantage of a completely new start, no more evening work and no more Mr Paul Gerrard.

Gael immediately gave up her evenings with Laura and within three weeks, she and Sampson were married. They decided to remain in Eastingleigh until Sampson's retirement so that Gael could continue her work at the council. He provided her with a car and arranged for purchase of a new house on an estate just outside town. Gael temporarily moved to live in a hotel in the main street until the purchase had been completed. A married woman now, she had independence, comfort and security.
At first, she was able to occupy herself in Sampson's absence by enhancing the appearance of the house. Sampson readily provided money for curtains, pictures, ornaments and the sort of things guaranteed to provide a feminine touch that most men would never think of. This kept her busily looking, choosing and buying in the local shops.

After three months, she began to wonder if she had made a mistake. Sampson was away far more than she had anticipated. Although he telephoned her most days, she was restless. She now had little contact with her mother, no contact with her neighbours, rarely saw Laura and no longer enjoyed her job. Sampson understood and promised to do something about it when she telephoned him to relate her problems. She longed to be with him, truly believing he would find a solution, but in the meantime she still had the problem of Paul Gerrard.
Since her marriage, they had rarely spoken. When their paths at work had inevitably crossed, Gael had gone out of her way to keep conversation to the absolute minimum. Paul Gerrard had wanted to re-establish a relationship, only to be rebuffed. He had tried to harass her, even calling to speak with her at her home in the evening. Only her threat to call the police had stemmed his advances. He merely succeeded in increasing Gael's antagonism towards him. Late one Friday afternoon, in an impulsive act of revenge, he went to reception, told her to gather together all her personal things and without reason, dismissed her from her job.

Talking the situation over with Laura gave her comfort and assurance. Laura was nobody's fool and at once advised her to go over Paul

Gerrard's head. As Gael knew that the Chief Executive was out of the office until mid-week, Laura suggested that Gael appeal in the first instance to the Mayor, Councillor Walter Spedding.

On Monday morning, Gael telephoned to make an appointment with the Mayor. Walter Spedding had seen her many times when he had passed through reception, spoken to her often in her role as telephonist and recognised her to be an attractive, lively and very efficient employee. Despite knowing of her reputation outside of the office, he listened as she told him she wished to make a serious complaint about her dismissal by a senior officer of the council and would like first of all to seek his advice. The Mayor had a heavy schedule that day interviewing talented young people to determine the level of financial assistance to be awarded to help them achieve success in their specialist fields. It was one of his favourite duties and quite demanding but listening to Gael's seductive voice, he agreed to see her later that afternoon.

Gael made sure she was presentable for the occasion. She wore a smart, dark blue dress, not too short - high heels but not too high - subtly applied make-up, but not too lavish - with an expensive perfume and immaculately styled hair. She walked confidently into the Mayor's Parlour and immediately received the Mayor's rapt attention. He was worldly-wise and used to making up his own mind based on fact. But he was an older man who just like many before him was instantly transfixed by the alluring presence of this young woman. Weak at the knees, he could only listen with the odd sympathetic exclamation as she twisted him around her little finger. He would in any event have wished to help her but when he was informed that Paul Garrard was involved, his advice was a foregone conclusion.

The Mayor, in his final month of office, saw the chance for the council to be rid of this drunken tyrant once and for all if Gael's claims of his treatment towards her were confirmed.

Promising to take up her case personally he telephoned the Chief Executive on his return first thing on Wednesday morning. He related the complaint and instructed him to interview Paul Gerrard at once in the presence of the Personel Officer to ascertain the facts and report back. When asked to state the grounds for Gael's abrupt dismissal, Paul Gerrard could provide no satisfactory reason. Gael was immediately re-instated and Paul Gerrard given a final written warning as to his future conduct.

He was by now effectively isolated in his job. The new Chief Executive had relied heavily upon him to run the department and conduct day-to-day business whilst he spent time away promoting the area as an attractive location to set up business ventures. Such reliance could no longer be guaranteed. Paul Gerrard's chaotic lifestyle was reflected in the state of his office. Correspondence remained unread, cluttered randomly upon his desk or on top of filing cabinets. Important business deals had to be delayed when documents could not be found or requested replies had been overlooked.

Paul Gerrard's personal life was also descending into a living hell. Usually late for work then taking a three-hour lunch, he remained at the office until it was time to drive to his favourite pub for drinks and dinner. The landlord was used to him taking his seat at the bar, drinking heavily, ordering a meal in the restaurant and driving home only when the pub closed at eleven o'clock. Comments were often made about his ability or otherwise to drive but although he was recognised as being an alcoholic, nothing was ever done to curtail or prevent this regular routine.
Apart from the odd occasion in the mornings when he came into the kitchen late after oversleeping, he did not see or speak with his wife. By the time he arrived home late the worse for drink, she had retired to her separate bedroom. Weekends were no exception. He left home early to drive to a nearby town where he spent all day in various pubs, betting shops and clubs. It proved to be a heavy strain upon his limited finances. This, and his obsession with Gael, who continued to be a constant part of his thoughts, had reduced him to a level of depression he could neither understand nor cope with.

When Sampson next returned, he told Gael that he had arranged to bring forward his retirement to the end of the year and wanted her to come immediately to live at his home in Pirimos.
Sampson had told her much about Greece, shown her photographs of his village and she was eager to start a new life there. She resigned from her job at once and the house they had bought in Eastingleigh was advertised for sale.

Gael's first experience of Greece was a mixture of delight and disappointment. The weather was wonderful, the village charming and Sampson's family more than welcoming. The disappointment was the house. Like many of its type in Greece, it was in the style of an apartment. To reduce tax, it was incomplete with thick metal struts protruding through the roof.

Sampson had not explained to her that his parents lived on the ground floor and his sister, brother-in-law and their three small children on the first floor. She and Sampson had three rooms on the partly completed second floor. Gael tried her best to adapt to her new situation but in many ways it resembled the cramped conditions and noisy household atmosphere she had so desperately tried to leave behind in her early teens. After only a few months, she informed Sampson that she was returning to their still unsold house in Eastingleigh to think things over.

Whilst thinking about her future, she met some of her old office colleagues and was told that her former post had once more become vacant. Straight away, she went to see the Chief Executive asking if it were possible that she be re-appointed.

In Gael's absence, Paul Gerrard had re-assessed his situation. Her departure overseas abruptly brought home to him the realisation that their past association was over for good. Slowly, this had the effect of reducing his depressed state as he realised he could live without her. He took his duties seriously, arriving earlier at the office and trying to reduce his lunchtime drinking habit. His health improved as he attempted desperately to cut out previous excesses, even leaving the pub to return home earlier in the evenings, much to the chagrin of his wife who had become used to having the house virtually to herself. But his home-life situation had been the same for years. He could handle that and now he was on course for a more normal life.

When Paul Gerrard heard that Gael had returned to Eastingleigh and that the Chief Executive had agreed to re-employ her, he was livid. He went straight across to the Chief Executive's office and thrust a letter into his hand that contained his ultimatum - either she goes or I resign!

As he stood there, arms folded, waiting for the Chief Executive to finish reading his letter, he was shocked to be told in no uncertain terms that his resignation was accepted. Under the Chief Executive's watchful eye, he was given five minutes to hand over all keys and effects that were council property and to clear his desk. Any remaining personal items would be forwarded on to him.

That afternoon, witnessed by the Mayor, Councillor Walter Spedding, the Chief Executive cleared Paul Gerrard's office. Despite knowing of Gerrard's problem, both were amazed at the amount of alcohol secreted in various drawers and cupboards.

"His own personal stock is far greater than the modest supply provided to the Mayor's Parlour for hospitality purposes," remarked Spedding.

"In many ways, I'm surprised your predecessor's didn't do something about this long ago. Local Government seems to give priority to people's rights rather than take action over their wrongdoings. If Gerrard had acted like that in the private sector and been allowed to stay, the business would have gone bankrupt."

Gael re-started her job the very next day and the vacant post of Deputy Chief Executive was advertised in both local and national journals.

Gael had been in post less than a month when two significant things occurred. First of all, the estate agency rang to say that an offer had been received on her and Sampson's house.

That weekend, Sampson arrived unexpectedly with news that his retirement terms had been agreed and accepted. With his lump sum and proceeds from sale of their house they would have more than sufficient to buy a separate property for them in his home village. Gael immediately resigned, happily resolved to spend her life with her husband in Greece.

In the meantime, Paul Gerrard had been perusing the legal sector job situations. He soon realised that few suitable posts were available and at over fifty years of age, he was not best placed to attract prospective employers' attentions.

When he heard that Gael had resigned to return to her husband, he felt a great surge of relief. His post had not yet been filled and next morning he left home early and went to see the Chief Executive. Confident that his past experience of the post would guarantee his return, he demanded re-instatement.

The Chief Executive gave him a withering look, telling him that an excellent short-list had been drawn up and that an appointment was imminent. Paul Gerrard would certainly not be added to that short-list. His depressed state was intensified. He spent a large part of his days unsuccessfully applying for jobs and the rest in various hostelries in the vicinity. Now without income, his bank overdraft soared. He attempted to overcome his misery through drink and gambling.

One winter's night, he left his favourite pub after an evenings drinking to drive home as usual. On the way, he vaguely recalled having felt his vehicle lurch to the right but had been able to control it, continuing on to park it in his garage. Next morning, he noticed that the offside front wing of his red car was badly damaged.

Late the previous evening, a passing motorist had observed a blue saloon car with headlights full on, resting upside down in a ditch at the side of the road, two miles from Paul Gerrard's home. An ambulance was called and two elderly occupants transported to hospital where both were detained for treatment, the lady passenger being in a serious condition. Police immediately informed all garages to be on the look out for any damaged red vehicle bearing blue paint marks brought in for repair.

When that afternoon Paul Gerrard drove his car down to the local garage to obtain an estimate, he was told to wait whilst damage was assessed. The garage owner rang the police and Paul Gerrard was taken to the police station for questioning. Although both breath and blood tests by this time recorded his blood alcohol content to be below the maximum legal level, he was eventually cautioned, charged with causing an accident by dangerous driving and failing to report it. He was allowed to consult a solicitor before being asked to sign a charge sheet and bailed to attend court at a future date.

A week later, his solicitor contacted him urgently to relay news that the elderly lady passenger had died and that he would most likely be charged with causing death by dangerous driving, possibly meaning a lengthy prison sentence.

That evening, in an angry and aggressive mood, he engaged in a bout of drinking causing his wife to leave the house to take refuge with her friend, Patrick Harper.

Later, Paul Gerrard went out for a walk wearing his overcoat with a scarf around his neck as protection against the bitterly cold night air.

Early next morning, the Ambulance Service received a '999' call from Mrs Gerrard. They arrived fifteen minutes later to find Mrs Gerrard and her friend Patrick Harper crouching over the dead body of Paul Gerrard, lying face upward on the floor of the integral garage.

Mrs Gerrard claimed that upon returning home from Patrick Harper's at around midnight, there had been no sign of her husband and she had gone straight to bed, locking her door. The following morning, she had been horrified to find her husband's body limply hanging by the neck attached to a rope secured to the garage roof beams. An overturned kitchen chair was on its side a couple of feet away.

Mrs Gerrard had hysterically explained that after phoning for the ambulance, she had run down the road in panic to Patrick Harper and beseeched him to come to her help. They had returned to the garage and between them, released Paul Gerrard's body from the rope attached to his neck, took off his scarf and overcoat, placing his body on the floor in a desperate but futile attempt to revive him.

At the inquest, the post mortem revealed that Paul Gerrard had perished as a result of asphyxia but was unable to state whether the cause was due to strangulation or hanging. When examined, it was apparent that Paul Gerrard had been dead for at least nine hours but that the rope impression on his neck did not appear to have the usual gap at the suspension point. In the absence of firm evidence, the Coroner concluded that Paul Gerrard had taken his own life as a result of recent problems associated with his personal situation.

After the trauma surrounding her husband's death, Mrs Gerrard found she was unable to continue living in the family home and moved to live with Patrick Harper. The house was eventually sold. She had an unpleasant surprise when realising that the proceeds and widows lump sum were insufficient to meet Paul Gerrard's substantial debts. Mrs Gerrard was left in reduced circumstances with just her widows pension.

After a respectable period of time, Patrick Harper retired selling both his business and house, when he paid off the residue of Paul Gerrard's debts. The couple were quietly married, moving to live in a rural village along the coast some distance from Eastingleigh. Although they both continued to inwardly relive the events leading up to Paul Gerrard's death, they never spoke of it. The subject was closed forever. It was their shared unspoken secret as they lived out the rest of their lives in the peace and tranquillity of the countryside.

BUGGIN'S TURN

The system of appointing people to positions based on rotation rather than merit. Buggin's isn't a real person, but one of the generic names, such as John Smith, used to define the typical man in the street. Many mayors of English towns and cities have long been selected in this way. Each year, a new mayor is appointed by simply choosing the next in line of the current body of elected councillors.

John Lenoir's inauspicious start to life belied a future that would see him chosen as mayor of his home town fifty-one years later. His unplanned birth in 1948 was the result of his mother's liaison with a farmer's son from a small village on the outskirts of Arras in Northern France. Straight out of the sixth form of Chevesley High School for Girls in Kent, she had gone on a summer hitch-hiking holiday and met his father when he had stopped to give her a lift. With a little English, he had been able to converse. On holiday himself, they subsequently spent two weeks together, camping in the Auvergne.

So infatuated was he that on the journey back to Calais, he had taken her to meet his parents in whose house she had spent the night before returning to England.

The couple corresponded regularly. When it became known that she was pregnant, both families, as was the custom in those days, made plans for their marriage. There was no question about it.

Her parents insisted that the child be born in England, after which his mother took John to live with his father's family on their farm in France. Although she tried hard to adapt to French culture, lack of the language prevented enjoyment of an integrated life. Her husband worked long hours and proved to have a problem with alcohol, causing her to became increasingly isolated. The marriage was ill starred, lasting only nine years before final, acrimonious divorce.

John had a clear recollection of his French upbringing. The formative years at *école maternelle,* French language, characteristics and rural life, weekend outings with his French grandparents, his father's hard working and equally hard drinking life - all were firmly implanted in his mind.

As the divorce proceeded, his mother returned with him to live with his English grandparents in Chevesley. Eventually, as an unemployed single mother in cramped accommodation without financial support from her husband, she was awarded one of the spacious but uncared for council houses in the Havelock ward of town. Then a neglected area of the borough, John's upbringing had been tough, accentuated by his being thrust into the English speaking educational system. Fortunately, English had always been the first language at home, so although initially struggling, he was soon able to cope admirably. After two years of financial wrangling, all alimony claims against his father were dropped, subject to him paying for John's further education.

Encouraged by both his mother and grandparents, he progressed sufficiently to merit a place at Chevesley High School for Boys. There, he was like a fish out of water. Chevesley was a prosperous town with many fine buildings and houses. Founded in early Victorian times, the school had a tradition of academic success and there was an element of intellectual snobbery attached to it. John was one of the very few pupils living in council accommodation, one of a minority whose households did not possess a car and, in that era, one of the very few without a father at home to support him.

His mother could never afford to send him to summer camp, on school trips abroad or buy him expensive equipment for recreational activities. He consequently displayed no enthusiasm for sport and made no real friends. In later life, he realised that this situation had not been totally disadvantageous, as it had enabled him to be sent in the long summer holidays to stay with his French grandparents, keep in contact with his father and improve his French conversation.

In term time, without the distraction of firm friendships or recreational activities, he concentrated upon his studies. His aptitude for figures enabled him to rise above adversity to obtain a mathematics degree at University. There, he developed an interest in politics and became an enthusiastic member of the debating society where his firebrand type of left-wing rhetoric was highly acclaimed by his growing band of supporters.

High school and University life had changed John for the better. Once a shy, retiring individual, he now cut an impressive figure. Six feet two inches tall with a large, if somewhat rotund, unathletic frame, he possessed a fine head of dark hair and piercing brown eyes. His face displayed a permanent quizzical expression as though expecting to have to answer a difficult question at any moment. A firm, welcoming handshake invariably put people at ease. With a deep, clear commanding voice, he liked nothing better than a night out, smoking and drinking with acquaintances and earnestly discussing world events. John had formed very clear opinions and was a persuasive advocate in support of his convictions.

Although mathematics was his subject, geography and history had always fascinated him. He took a year out to visit as many countries as time and finance would allow. Journeys to Russia and eastern bloc countries further encouraged his interest in politics. Deeply moved by the plight of the proletariat before the revolution and their subsequent suppression during the cold war years, it seemed natural to him, in the absence of a Communist alternative, to look to the Labour Party as a source of enlightenment.

Upon his return, he soon obtained his first teaching post as mathematics teacher at Rathgate Secondary Modern School, situated in an industrial town a few miles from Chevesley. Shortly afterwards, he applied to join the local Chevesley branch of the Labour Party whose headquarters were in his home ward of Havelock.
Having been accepted and paid his membership subscription, he endeavoured to encourage the local party, attending meetings, distributing pamphlets on behalf of election candidates and helping in any way he could. A dedicated activist and a powerful speaker in support of the cause, he gained a reputation as something of a reactionary, a constant supporter of redistribution of wealth, protection against what he saw as exploitation of the working class, reduction of their working hours and payment of a living wage. For his pains he was frequently addressed as 'Comrade John'.
In many ways, his was a thankless task. The local council, Chevesley Borough, had fifty-five members; eleven wards returning two members

and a further eleven returning three. His own ward of Havelock was the only left-wing stronghold, returning both of the boroughs two Labour Party members. Conservatives had a large majority, the remainder being Liberal or Independent councillors.

During the late 1970s, still living at home with his mother, they had argued about the merits of home ownership. John was vehemently opposed to the council's 'right to buy' scheme and dismayed when told she had signed to purchase the house at a substantial discount. She, of all people should have realised that they would not be in their present position if there had been a shortage of available, affordable housing to rent, but now there would be one less. It made him even more determined to achieve his social goals.

Rathgate Secondary Modern School proved to be an ideal environment for John to start his career. The majority of pupils were from backgrounds all too familiar to him; broken homes, households without employment or with low incomes and living in basic, rented accommodation. There were many difficult, disadvantaged children to deal with but also some underachievers and late developers. Whatever their social or educational deficiencies, for a dozen exhausting years, John tried to instil in them a desire for improvement; an ambition that might one day lead to fulfilment in life.

His diligent work at Rathgate was widely recognised and when a post of mathematics teacher became vacant at his old school, Chevesley High School for Boys, he was encouraged by his headmaster to apply.

It was a hard choice. John enjoyed the challenge of trying to help less fortunate children to find a role in life. He was comfortable working with them, could relate to their problems and had gained their respect.

However he was also aware, coming from a working class background, the surest way to improve was to take opportunities that came along. The lure of working at his old school proved irresistible. He saw himself as just the person to change the schools historic, outmoded traditions and bring it into the twentieth century.

With a sound recommendation, his undoubted mathematical ability and proven communication skills, he was welcomed back to Chevesley High School for Boys after a gap of sixteen years.

During that time, much to his satisfaction, John found that the school had already undergone considerable change. In his day, all teachers without exception were male. Now, woman accounted for half. Pupils of mixed race had superseded the former classes of all-white pupils whose only language was English. Where once, his surname, Lenoir, had been the only foreign sounding one in the whole school, the current register represented the directory of a league of nations At his first mathematics lesson, twelve of his class of thirty did not speak English as their first language. This situation had been one of the strengths of his experience at Rathgate and the main reason he had been appointed.

But Chevesley High School for Boys remained a school for the elite and wealthy. Children dropped off by parents driving brand new four by fours, no doubt, thought John, having arranged for some dubious tax avoidance scheme to pay for the vehicles. Even the upper sixth form boys drove to lessons in cars far superior to his old, second-hand model. There was still much to teach them about the less fortunate members of society.

John settled quickly into his post and, with his French language ability, was able to stand in more than adequately in the absence of one or other of the two French teachers. A natural French speaker, his accent was better than either of theirs and in class, pupils preferred his practical approach to the more textbook lessons they normally received. This became common knowledge to other teachers including the headmaster, but did not enamour him to his two colleagues.

As his career in school flourished, so too did his political ambitions. When one of the sitting Labour members for Havelock announced his retirement, John immediately applied for and was selected as prospective candidate for the vacant seat. In the run up to the subsequent election, his ability to speak coherently and persuasively at public meetings throughout the ward saw him easily hold the seat for his party.

By now familiar with the style and traditions of local government, he regarded them as mirroring his school's ethos - privileged and out of touch with the modern world. Yet, as one of only two Labour members, his ability to influence and ring the changes was severely limited. He could observe, comment and propose without the power to transform. At the bottom of the ladder, he had nevertheless established a first foothold within the local government hierarchy and if he continued to retain his seat, the future promised gradual progression.

John directed his energies towards the welfare of his constituents securing appointment to both the council's housing and social services committees. His objective was to promote the increase in the supply of social housing, application of fair rents and distribution of necessary benefits to the needy.

Success in both work and politics soon brought conflicting interests to the surface. Several council committee meetings were held in the afternoon, requiring other teachers to cover for mathematics lessons in John's absence. John always prepared comprehensive notes for stand-in teachers but, in their opinion, attempting to teach an unfamiliar subject was difficult and did not benefit pupils. In truth, it wasn't lack of information that irked them most but the fact that they had to take extra lessons without pay!

Included on the Board of Governors was a teacher's representative who was instructed by the staff to ask the Board to either refuse John permission to be absent on council affairs or pay them to cover for him. The headmaster and other class-conscious governors fully supported John. Despite his known political leanings, his absences were viewed as beneficial to the school. Having an elected councillor within their ranks was considered advantageous when discussing important future subjects such as charity relief, grants, planning and development permissions.To emphasise the point, the school prospectus included a brief note referring to the excellent relationship the school had forged with the town's local administration. Another quality in John's favour was his ability to tutor sixth form students in the mathematical logic of STEP (Sixth Term Examination Paper) at all three levels. As universities progressively demanded ever-higher entry standards a STEP pass mark became essential and John's input enabled the school to boast success in the number of pupils gaining entry to Cambridge and other top universities. The headmaster also had a tacit regard for John's firm stance in dealing directly with the often venomous complaints of irate, pushy parents. John somehow had the knack of telling them to the effect that their progeny were not precious potential protégés but simply pampered, lazy little parasites.

The headmaster often wished that more of his teaching staff had some of John's courage and incisiveness.

John's mother never remarried and as the years passed, he continued to live with her in their former council house. They had long overcome their difference of opinion on the purchase and she was the most loving and loyal supporter of his dual roles in teaching and politics. Although he would never publicly admit to it, he had gradually come to terms with the working environment in an elitist school. Much opposed to central government interference in education and the growing emphasis on league tables, he did his utmost to balance time off from mathematics lessons with extra cover for French and STEP tuition. The school had a reputation for excellence and he wished to be seen to be fully contributing to it and its pupil's successes.

Having gone on to win four successive local elections, John became the longest serving Labour member on the council. Teaching staff resentment reached new heights when it was rumoured that John was in line to become mayor of the borough. Sixteen years a council member, the title was bestowed not upon party lines, but by seniority. If a councillor by length of service was next in line, then *'buggin's turn'* applied and that person duly chosen. Never, in the long history of the borough's charter, dating back to the Middle Ages, had anyone from the Labour Party held the title.

In earlier years, John would have decried the position as ceremonial humbug. His view then was that the role and all the trappings that came with it were irrelevant in a modern society and could be simply carried out by an elected chairman. He had thought the ritual of donning the long, red, fur-lined robe and wearing the heavy gold chain of office bad enough, but the sight of someone wearing a tricorn hat seemed faintly ridiculous. The practice of parading through town in full regalia accompanied by an entourage of present and past mayors of adjacent authorities for a service of dedication, conducted by an appointed mayor's chaplain, seemed even more ludicrous.

Still, acceptance of his role as a professional teacher in an elitist school had helped him to understand the long established customs of local administration. The status of mayor was viewed as an appointment resulting from successful achievements and the honour widely coveted. The surrounding pomp and traditions were an integral part of history, a subject he professed to appreciate. His experience told him that the incumbent could fully embrace the role without compromising his or her principles. John had always possessed radical ideas but he was not an anarchist.

By 1998, several Conservative, Liberal and Independent members had accumulated more service than John but only one had not had the honour of becoming mayor. Therefore, under *'buggin's turn'*, John was in line to be chosen for the coveted position of mayor in the Millennium year 1999/2000. Few had thought that 'Comrade John' with his far left leanings would even consider the office and were surprised when he expressed his desire to become the town's foremost representative. It was his one chance and if he rejected it he might not have another opportunity.

One seemingly small hurdle stood in John's path. In May1998, he was due to stand for re-election. His four previous victories had been by comfortable majorities but of some concern was the recent increase in Labour councillors to five members. His ward and increasingly others, like his school pupils, now comprised of many immigrants - often talented, qualified, professional people with young families intent upon making their mark on society. John's continued defence and promotion of traditional socialist values marked him to some to be a man slipping out of touch with local community and party aspirations. The modern breed of socialist was perceived by John to be more interested in self-promotion than improving conditions for the socially disadvantaged. These ambitious politicians, adept at manipulating people and policies to achieve personal objectives, had progressively infiltrated the party. Their cravings for change extended far beyond petty jealousies. They wanted total power and brooked no opposition. They did not speak in the same compassionate terms as John and to him, were little different from Communist dictators. Having successfully targeted certain seats, devious and divisive political undercurrents were circulating against John's interests. It was his seat they were now aiming for. The knives were out. One evening John was called before a small party caucus for what was ostensibly a meeting to rubber stamp his candidature to defend his seat in the forthcoming election. With a minimum quorum, they voted that he be replaced by one of their like-minded number as Labour candidate. His real enemies had proven not to be opposition party members but so-called colleagues within his own team. It was clear that failure to toe the party line with this new species of Labour hierarchy resulted in summary rejection.

Such scheming and treachery roused John to action. Those naïve would-be power-brokers could play their own mind games, but he would have no part of it. Accordingly, he resigned from the party and announced that he would contest his Havelock ward seat as an Independent Labour candidate.

Faced by strong opposition from an official Labour candidate aided by both party funding and administrative backing, and with opportunist Conservative and Liberals sensing a possible killing, John, was none to confident of success.

He hadn't fully realised the extent of grass-roots Labour support for his type of politics. Standing as an Independent Labour candidate in his own Havelock ward, he received assistance from many disillusioned electors who had faithfully voted for him over the years. With careful planning, they carried out house-to-house canvassing and contacted as many registered voters as possible. Never one to embrace technology, John continued to rely upon the personal touch, composing, printing and helping deliver over four thousand copies of his manifesto. When his local campaign group reported that they were receiving many pledges of support, he remained unconvinced, knowing from experience that doorstep pledges did not always translate into votes.

He and his team were therefore astonished when the result was announced. John had received more votes than the combined total of the other three candidates!

Returned for a further four years, John joined all other members in supporting the proposal that the next councillor in line be selected as mayor for 1998/99 and confidently awaited his turn for the forthcoming Millennium. In preparation for what promised to be a busy year ahead, he reduced to a minimum his time off from teaching mathematics and from a distance observed the current mayor fulfilling his duties. John was amused to be told that, following a town-twinning visit to France, the mayor had unwittingly made a *'faux pas'*. Having enjoyed the generous hospitality of the host twinning committee and the lively company of the attractive lady *maire*, he had written to thank her in his rudimentary French. The letter ended - *"La prochain fois que nous nous rencontrons, je vais te baiser"* - meaning to say that next time they met he would kiss her. In the nuance of the French language, he had failed to realise that the use of *'baiser'* was risky, commonly interpreted in the vulgar sense of 'to screw'. When told of how his sentiments had been translated, an embarrassed mayor had asked John to personally telephone the lady *maire* to offer his profound apologies. Anticipating a short, frosty response, the mayor had listened in to the surprisingly long, apparently light-hearted conversation at the end of which, John was able to tell him that she had been amused and flattered by his letter, that no offence had been taken and next time would he please use the verb *'embrasser'*.

Following the May 1999 elections, the new council convened to choose the Millennium mayor. John, as the longest serving member was duly proposed but contrary to the usual unanimous approval, the four remaining Labour Party members named one of their number, citing that the *'Buggin's turn'* method did not necessarily provide the most competent leader. No one, they claimed, had the right to automatic selection and they called upon members to discontinue this undemocratic system in favour of a secret ballot. If John had ever had any lingering reservations about acceptance, they were now totally dispelled. Following a heated discussion, the outgoing Conservative mayor, grateful for John's intervention over his twinning visit gaffe, confirmed his support for the existing method, called for a show of hands for the proposal of John as mayor, ensuring his party and most of the other councillors raised their hands in support.

John had no qualms about fully embracing the role. His inaugural ceremony as Mayor took place on a warm Sunday morning in May. Never having married, he was proud to have the assistance of his mother as Lady Mayoress.
Fitted for the mayoral robe, wearing the tricorn hat, with the heavy, glittering, gold chain of office around his neck, he took his place at the

head of the long procession. Among those attending were other local mayors, many councillors and his school's Board of Governors. Notable absentees were the four Labour Party members and several of his school's teaching staff, having taken the decision to boycott the event. The procession threaded its way through town towards Havelock Parish Church for a service conducted by the Chaplain of his school.

Later that week, John took the chair at the first meeting of the Millennium year. John had dressed in the mayor's parlour, situated at the end of a long, wide, high ceilinged corridor leading to the council chamber. Once he had finished dressing, he followed his uniformed attendant out into the corridor. As they walked slowly along, John stopped to gaze at the portraits and photographs of many past mayors of the borough. They represented a large number of influential people who had contributed much to the town - landed gentry, captains of industry and philanthropists. The realisation that he, 'Comrade John' was about to join that eminent gallery was a humbling experience.

Assembled council members and chief officers stood to attention as the mayor's attendant threw open the doors of the council chamber to the loud proclamation :-

'Be upstanding for His Worshipful,
the Mayor of Chevesley Borough Council'.

There was a respectful silence as John entered the chamber and took his place at the elevated, ornate, high-backed chair at the top table reserved for the chairman. His Chaplain rose to deliver a short prayer, wishing John divine guidance throughout his year of office and wisdom to members in general in their decision-making processes. After thanking the Chaplain for his ministrations, John immediately set the tone for his mayoralty. His style of leadership was characterised by reorganisation of mayoral duties. Outside of school holidays, all but the most important daytime events were delegated to his more than willing deputy. He attended no afternoon committee meetings. During weekdays, he used the mayor's car sparingly. His appearances were concentrated upon evenings and weekends. He knew that he must not neglect his teaching career for, as an Independent Labour councillor at the next election, he was far from certain to retain the seat. With his forthright style, political experience and genial manner, John lived up to his reputation of being firm but fair. At formal council meetings, he proved adept at controlling debates and knowing the right moment to ask members to vote upon a particular proposal. His approach was even-handed. He upheld the dignity of the mayoral role, even allowing limited scope for his former Labour Party allies to voice their views even when he was personally vehemently opposed to them. He ensured that officers' reports were factual and members' comments succinct. At social events, he was in his element, with a natural ability to find appropriate words to match the occasion. He spoke at official functions; presented prizes; attended galas and met visiting dignitaries. The Millennium celebrations included a party for pensioners in the Town Hall with a traditional jazz band and a generous buffet provided at John's personal expense.

One of his final duties as mayor was to receive a delegation from the French twinning town. He took great delight in introducing himself to '*Madame le Maire*' in perfect French and kissing her. There was no misunderstanding this time.

He took her on a conducted tour of the Town Hall and they stood before the large oak 'honours boards'. Etched in gold lettering were the names of each mayor of the borough from the Middle Ages. Recorded there were Colonels and Majors from long ago wartime battles; Knights and Dames of the realm; Aldermen; doctors of various fields of knowledge; MBEs; CBEs and OBEs. Down at the very foot of the last board was recorded just plain 'JOHN LENOIR', 1999/2000, the last mayor of that era but certainly not the least.

POSTSCRIPT

John's active year as mayor took its toll on his health. A lover of good food and drink, he was cognisant of the fate of his father who had died aged forty-three of an alcohol related illness. John had had every intention of regulating his diet but the regular formal lunches, afternoon teas and dinners had proved irresistible. He had added weight and consumed far too much wine when confronted by the abundant hospitality of his many hosts. Additionally, upon relinquishing the mayoralty, he had, as was the case with many of his predecessors, felt the type of depression associated with sudden change and loss of power. He struggled through his teaching duties until end of term, then spent the whole summer under doctor's orders recuperating. The sense of loss was acute, made worse by enforced absence from his beloved Labour Party. Favourable treatment he might have given to his former Labour colleagues, but the hoped for reconciliation and invitation to rejoin the party was not forthcoming. Resentment of his success in the Havelock ward as an Independent Labour member ran deep. His desire to once again represent them as an official candidate was dashed. He had three more years to serve, and then he was at the mercy of the unforgiving political system.

Chevesley High School for Boys also underwent significant change. The Headmaster retired after a long and distinguished career and with his departure went John's chief ally. The new Headmaster, in accordance with teaching staff's wishes reduced John's absences on council business to the absolute minimum. With increasing paperwork, school inspection and top-heavy officialdom, teaching had turned from a joy to an unrewarding task. John made strenuous efforts to adjust and deal efficiently with new initiatives but to no avail. When, a year later an offer of early retirement presented itself, John reluctantly accepted and left the school aged only fifty-four. He had never thought for one moment that he would ever be forced to consider such an option but in his judgement, teaching had become a political football; teachers were never asked for their views, never listened to and never allowed to be just teachers. The job was stressful and he was better off out of it.

He still had his local council seat and was reflecting on the possibilities of defending it as an Independent candidate. His mother's sudden death effectively ended any such notions. Having relied upon her love and support since childhood, he was devastated. It was only the sympathy and encouragement he received from his many supporters that prevented him from instantly resigning the seat.

His fighting spirit pulled him through but with a staunch working class background, he experienced great embarrassment when his mother's house was valued as part of her estate. Being a substantially built 1930s former council property, now fully modernised and situated in a gentrified, sought after area of Southern England, it was assessed at half a million pounds. Faced with a substantial inheritance tax bill John was forced to sell and move to a modest flat in the centre of town.

It was at this point that his life took a turn for the better. One of his faithfully Labour party supporters, Joyce, a widow in her sixties had long been a voluntary worker with the Citizens Advice Bureau. She had great admiration for his unstinting efforts to help the disadvantaged and urged him to speak with the local Director to offer his services. Appreciating the uncertainties of politics and that Independent councillors often only last one term of office, John was delighted to accept the Directors offer for him to join the team for three days a week on an expenses only basis. He started at once and found the job a true eye-opener. As a councillor for eighteen years he had rarely came across so many cases of social injustice and administrative incompetence. His knowledge of local government systems and links with councillors and staff proved invaluable in helping successfully rectify many of the problems presented to him. In this face-to-face role with people in need, he was more effective than being a member of the council. It became for him an easy decision not to contest the Havelock ward seat at the next election.

The success rate at Chevesley High School for Boys had slipped since John's departure. None of the existing mathematics teachers had John's competences in coaching university hopefuls in the required STEP papers. The school had got into the frame of mind that just because students were going to get 3A*s, they were sure of a place at a top university. They failed to understand what was required and did not offer special tuition. When students looked at their first STEP paper a few months before the examination, they realised they should have been receiving tuition earlier. When submitting their university options, they were unable to nominate two top universities for fear of failure and being consigned to the subsequent lottery for a place at a university of lesser standing.
Having knowledge of John's ability in STEP coaching, desperate students and panicking parents on behalf of their children began to request his help.
His flat in the centre of town had a large drawing room and, as his reputation grew, he began to organise full day classes at weekends. Joyce helped him set up a web site setting out his qualifications, experience and teaching rates. Once he had started, with the field to himself, he was surprised to find that students were prepared to pay the substantial fees

Joyce had told him were the norm. His courses were usually oversubscribed with students willing to travel many miles to his home, such was the clamour to obtain the desired grades.

John had enjoyed most of his teaching career and had reached the ultimate pinnacle of being mayor of his home town. Although much of that time had been stressful - resentment from other teachers, enmity from members of his own party - 'Comrade John' had come a long way over the years and received a practical education himself. He had never made money from being a councillor or mayor, claiming only expenses actually incurred. In discussions involving his constituents or his school, he had, when necessary, always declared an interest and left the debating chamber, leaving others to make the decision without any undue influence on his part. The windfall profit from the sale of his late mother's house had been fortuitous and had helped offset the reduction in his anticipated final pension lump sum. He was not a rich man but through hard work, determination and skill, was comfortable and content. Now he had the best of both worlds. The ability to help the poorer members of society often incapable of helping themselves and assisting promising young students to achieve their ambitions in the comfort of his own home.

Following the challenge to John's status as next in line to be mayor of the borough, councillors consigned the system of *'Buggin's turn'* to history. Political dominance would henceforth prevail. John was sad to see the end of *'Buggin's'* that had been brought about by the intransigence of his Labour Party enemies. But with minority representation, it was highly unlikely that a Labour Party member would be chosen to be mayor of Chevesley Borough Council.
John's year of office would likely remain the only one held by a Labour member. He was justly proud of that.

Hector Garcia's sister's seafood paella

TOWN TWINNING FARCE

Farce

A comic dramatic piece that uses highly improbable situations, stereotyped characters, extravagant exaggeration and violent horseplay. It is generally considered inferior to comedy in its crude characterisations and implausible plots but it has been sustained by its popularity in performance and has persisted throughout the Western World to the present day.

It sometimes happens that a chance meeting arising from unlikely circumstances develops into much more than a passing event. So it was in the case of Alberto Sanchez and Kathleen Redfern when their marriage in 1945 was the catalyst to the twinning of their respective towns.

Alberto had been born in the Northern Spanish town of Iguderra and in his early twenties, fighting against the fascist Franco forces in the Spanish Civil War, was captured and tortured. He managed to escape and with the aid of sympathisers made his way over the Pyrénées into France, then across to England. He vowed never to return to Spain whilst Franco was in power. His misfortunes were compounded when having found the tranquil calm of England, the onset of the Second World War saw him interned as a foreign alien in the Midlands town of Abberford.

Kathleen lived with her widowed mother not far from the camp where Alberto was confined and each day saw the interns pass by on their daily exercise routine. Feeling sorry for their situation she regularly supplied them with cigarettes. She found herself looking out especially for Alberto who despite having no English always smiled gratefully at her for the gifts she gave them. Eventually she plucked up courage to request authorisation from the camp authorities for Alberto to be allowed to visit her and her mother for tea. Permission was given and despite Alberto's obvious shyness in what were unfamiliar surroundings, the arrangement continued throughout the war years. Their friendship developed and at the onset of peace, they were married.

With little money available none of Alberto's family were able to make the journey to England and it was therefore a quiet wedding in Abberford Catholic Church.

Alberto's refusal to recognise the Franco regime prevented a return to Spain and the families did not meet until 1953 when Alberto's parents made their first visit to England. Alberto's father was at the time *Alkatea* (equivalent to the title of Mayor) of Iguderra and as such, Kathleen arranged for him to meet the Mayor of Abberford. At that period in history, the concept of pairing towns, especially in Europe was seen as a way of fostering human and cultural links among nations and promoting international peace and understanding. Both towns had a similar population, an historic link with the textile industry and by 1954 a twinning agreement had been forged, a first for both towns. For the next forty-nine years there had been an annual cultural exchange. For the fiftieth anniversary, it was Iguderra's turn to host events.

As time had progressed the commonality between the two towns had evaporated with the demise of factory life, as jobs were increasingly lost to lower paid workers in the Far East. The skyline of Abberford no longer bristled with tall factory chimneys, the Victorian edifices having been demolished and replaced by a multiplicity of light engineering and commercial business parks. Iguderra on the other hand, being situated on the coast had been able to transform itself into a modern, thriving holiday destination thanks to the dawn of cheap package holidays in the 1960s. The towns were now so unalike as to provide an interesting contrast.
Both parties eagerly anticipated the four - day visit of eighty residents of Abberford to Iguderra. It was set to be a joyous occasion, a celebration and confirmation of the strong mutual respect for the dignity of both the towns and their countries. Having been twinning members from the outset, Alberto and Kathleen, now in their mid seventies had made their own travel arrangements, anticipating that it would be the highlight of their year. It would mark Antonio's return to the town of his birth, making it a special and memorable occasion for them both. Of that they had no doubt.

Just as the topography of both towns had changed dramatically, so too had the demographic and political structures.

After the war, the staunchly Socialist town of Iguderra saw the closure of its factories with alarming rapidity. Unemployment soared to over a quarter of the population and despite the best efforts of local politicians, promised inward investment failed to materialise. Many young people deserted the town for better prospects in the cities or overseas. The saviour for the town and the region proved to be the local airport that had been extensively used during the Civil War and was still in good condition. When a British travel company made overtures to use the airport for tourism purposes the authorities, with commendable vision, foresaw the prospect of new jobs and income for the area. A trial period of two years was agreed based on free use of the airport and its facilities. The trial proved to be so successful that the only problem was the lack of accommodation for the number of holidaymakers who clamoured to book inexpensive flights. With government and regional backing, financial and planning conditions were developed to enable a swift expansion of necessary hotels, apartments and support structures. Gradually, the number of flights increased and with the majority bringing tourists from British airports the numbers of English speaking people in the area increased dramatically. British investment was also encouraged and by the 1990s several of the hotels were British owned and operated as were a considerable number of restaurants, cafés and tourist shops. With over 200 hotels and many thousands of apartment units, the majority of townsfolk were now employed in tourism. Thanks to the combination of climate and special winter deals, this continued throughout the year. The old days of long hours of hard manual labour and strong unions had been transformed into a dynamic free enterprise culture headed by private enterprise fully supported by the Town Council. Council representation, previously dominated by the socialists was now under the control of the Basque Nationalist Party.

In the general election of 1951, Abberford had returned two right wing Conservatives to Parliament and the Conservatives held the local Town Council with a workable majority. The loss of textile factory jobs was not as swift as had been the case in Iguderra and the 1960s saw a large increase in foreign and commonwealth immigrants into the town on the prospects of a steady job, good pay, cheap housing in the predominantly two-bedroom terraces near the town centre and an improved standard of life. Such hopes were dashed by the 1980s by which time the factories had closed, unemployment had trebled and there was political and social unrest in the town. Recovery was slow but under the guidance of a newly formed Enterprise Zone that was able to access European funding, the town was gradually transformed into a centre of excellence for light engineering, employing both highly skilled and semi-skilled workers. As a consequence, many of the former residents were able to move to new housing developments outside of town. This, coupled with electoral boundary changes, saw a vast reduction in the Conservative vote so that by the mid 1990s, the town council had become a left wing stronghold.

Both towns started off the twinning arrangement in similar fashion by applying for a subvention from the local council to meet initial operational costs and ensure sufficient funds were available to promote the towns to their visitors. Neither town received nor indeed requested extravagant funding but advertised for membership of the twinning association based on a small annual subscription and the members' willingness to fund raise. In the early years, both towns received support from several hundred members, very few of whom could afford the biennial visit but who were prepared to host visitors in their own homes. After several years, many members of both twinning committees had formed permanent friendships with their hosts and it was taken for granted that the same people would, subject to availability, stay with the same hosts. As the population of both towns became more cosmopolitan, it was not unusual to find several British born couples now living and working permanently in Iguderra hosting families from Abberford on the premise that it overcame obvious language difficulties.

The *Alkatea* of Iguderra, in the final year of his four year term and Mayor of Abberford, in his single year of office had a shared objective. In the grand tradition of incumbents in a post of privilege and power for such a short term, they strove to implement some policy by which they would be remembered. As far as the twinning arrangement was concerned, the senior members of the twinning committee and official interpreters guided them. Previous Mayors had always been grateful for the help of their advisors and had been more than pleased to accept the arrangements made without question. They had their day to day responsibilities to attend to and felt comfortable leaving the twinning itinerary to those with experience of such matters. It had worked perfectly well before and there was no reason to suppose that it would not do so in future.

However, the twinning anniversary year of 2004 had thrown together a set of unpredictable circumstances. Since initial twinning, both towns had cemented arrangements with other towns, mainly European but some North African and formerly Russian territory. Iguderra now had links with towns in Tunisia, Germany and Latvia and Abberford with towns in Holland and Italy.

Hector Garcia, the elected *Alkatea* of Iguderra had decided that the fiftieth anniversary visit of Abberford would be the occasion of his legacy to the town. A spectacular event destined to be remembered forever in the annals of local political history.
Hector was a proud Spaniard and determined to show the world the importance of the town's rich Basque heritage. He had been born in the town some sixty-five years ago and Basque was his first language. He felt that it had been somewhat overshadowed in recent years with the influx of foreign tourists and was determined to put the record straight. He recognised that external investment had been beneficial to the town but his pride in being Basque and Spanish required reinforcement beyond doubt. A builder by trade he had benefited from the construction boom in the town. Many lucrative contracts had come his way and his firm had rapidly become one of the largest employers in the entire region. A big, swarthy, bluff, no nonsense character, strong as an ox and adept politically at

negotiating business deals, he was a man used to getting his own way. Now very rich, he considered himself financially independent and answerable to none.

Without any consultation, he wrote personally to the Mayor of Abberford inviting their twinning members presence in Iguderra to celebrate the fiftieth anniversary during the second week in September. He also wrote a similar invitation to the twinning groups of the other three towns, saying that this occasion was a landmark event, which would no doubt be repeated when their fiftieth anniversaries duly arrived. Acceptances quickly followed and the news was generally welcomed as a shrewd initiative by a cunning *Alkatea.*

The newly elected Mayor of Abberford was a local doctor, Tahir Solanki who had been born in Abberford of immigrant Indian parents from the Gujarat region. Ten years previously, he had been elected to the council as representative of one of the inner wards of the town. He was a consummate politician, had quickly become head of the ruling left wing Labour Party and elected mayor of the town for 2004. With a large Gujarati Indian population within his ward, his political future was secure. In his year of office he determined to promote their way of life as an example of the highest form of worldly culture.

He cut a slight figure, small, wiry, a thin moustache complimenting his lush main of jet black, silky hair. Against a dark skin, his even white teeth gave his smile an attractive, almost luminous quality. As a doctor and politician he considered himself to be on permanent duty and invariably wore a dark suit, shirt and tie. The sole exception was when attending official council functions when he regarded it as an honour to dress in the robes and chain of office. Relaxation and recreation were not recognisable features of his life. He had never been to Spain, knew little of its culture and was not disposed to ask the opinion of any of his colleagues who had experience of previous visits. He, as Mayor would be responsible for ensuring that his town was proactive in providing to the event its full share of cultural knowledge.

The rival ambitions of the two elected heads was not initially apparent and no one questioned the change of date to September from the usual May visit, nor the administration involving considerably more twinning visitors than the normal fifty or sixty. Not even Antonio and Kathleen Sanchez could have anticipated events as they arranged to fly to Iguderra and stay with Antonio's brother and his wife.

Hector Garcia's reason for changing the usual date of the twinning visit was, to him, quite simple. The second week in September was the town's *corrida* festival and as such, incorporated all things Basque and Spanish that Hector wished to promote.

'It will be an education for all our visitors', he had declared. There was no disagreement.

It only started to dawn upon Iguderra twinning committee members and their Spanish interpreters of the possible difficulties of organising this event when Hector Garcia had received acceptances from all four of Iguderra's invited twin towns, totalling approximately 260 people. It was immediately obvious that not only was their budget insufficient to finance such numbers but that it would be impossible to accommodate most of the visitors with their usual hosts. The *Alkatea* was unrepentant. Hector had not become a rich man by spending his own money.

'I shall demand an increase to my annual allowance and you must undertake more fund raising events and advertise for additional families to host our guests', was his response. 'This is a once in a lifetime opportunity to promote our history and culture to the world and we must take advantage of it'.

His influence over the Council was such that a contingency sum was immediately granted and the twinning committee members were able to persuade sufficient families and hoteliers to set aside enough rooms for the increased visitor numbers.

The panic seemed to be over when the programme of events, personally drawn up by Hector Garcia, was despatched to the twin towns. It was specifically designed to incorporate everything that the town stood for and as a stage for Hector to promote them.

Programme of Events

Friday	8 Sept	20.00	Welcome from Hector Garcia, *Alkatea,* Iguderra
		21.30	Celebration Dinner
Saturday	9 Sept	10.00	Full day visit to La Rioja wine harvest and festival
		22.00	Football Lliga 1 Iguderra v Bilbao
Sunday	10 Sept	14.30	Corrida de toros
Monday	11 Sept	10.30	Visit to Basque museum
		20.30	Flamenco and Fandango dinner/dance festival
Tuesday	12 Sept	11.30	Farewell speech from Hector Garcia.

The Mayor of Abberford, Tahir Solanki, received the programme appreciatively. As he read it, the item that drew his attention was the visit to the dance festival. He didn't give it too much consideration at the time but it slowly developed from a small piece of information in the back of his mind into an idea that appealed to him. Just two days before departure he picked up the telephone and asked how many people had signed up to visit Iguderra. He was told that two fifty-seat coaches had been booked to transport eighty people. That was just the answer he was seeking. The idea that had formed from his reading of the programme could now be put into effect. There were twenty empty seats, more than sufficient for his needs. Dancing was a spectacular form of culture in Gujarat and one that would promote its long standing traditions dating back to the ancient period of Lord Krishna. Tahir Solanki was chairman of the local Gujarati association and immediately decided that sixteen members of their School of Dance would accompany the twinning members to Iguderra.

"It won't cost any more for the coach if we carry eighty or ninty-six passengers. They do not need to pay as they will be dancing when they are in Iguderra as ambassadors for their parents country of birth," he decreed.

The coaches were due to leave Abberford early on Thursday afternoon to catch the overnight ferry from Portsmouth to Bilbao. The usual happy holiday atmosphere was stretched to the limit when the sixteen additional dancers arrived, each with two large suitcases. The baggage compartment contained presents for their hosts together with a large trunk into which the mayor had carefully packed his mayoral robes and chain of office. There was insufficient room to take additional luggage. The cases were too big to be placed in the coaches and much to the mayor's annoyance, their carefully packed ornate costumes had to be taken out, squashed unceremoniously into the overhead storage space and the suitcases left behind. With so little room available it was an uncomfortable journey to the south coast and everyone was relieved when the coaches eventually pulled into the quayside.

On arrival, the mayor was told that the cost of the sixteen extra passengers would amount to almost £1,600 and must be paid immediately. In his haste to implement his plan he hadn't realised that the coaches were only taking the group to Portsmouth from where they would board the ferry as foot passengers. Soon an argument ensued between the committee members, interpreter and mayor as to who would be held responsible for the costs. Practically, the only person with a credit card with sufficient allowance to cover this sum was the Mayor who held the council's credit card for emergency expenditure purposes. After persuasive arguing from everyone involved, the Mayor with bad grace eventually proffered the card for payment deciding that it was expenditure in the interests of official council business and thus perfectly legal!

They boarded the ferry and transferred their cases from the coaches with the beautiful dance costumes packed into hastily acquired large plastic bin bags.The sea crossing was uneventful and overnight sleep allowed tempers to cool. They disembarked in the early morning, were met by a hired coach and after breakfast, arrived at Iguderra by lunchtime.

The difficulties then began in earnest. All regular Abberford twinning members had been expecting to stay with their usual host families and were unaware that a further 150 people from the other twin towns were descending upon Iguderra. Many of the host families were regular hosts to members of the other twin towns and obviously the usual arrangements could not operate on this occasion. The majority of Abberfords members therefore disappointedly found that they had been allocated to families they had never met before or had been placed in a seaside hotel. In the hectic build-up to the trip, no one had thought fit to inform the Iguderra hosts of the extra sixteen dancers

Tahir Solanki and his wife were to be hosted by the Chief of Police and his wife. That turned out to be a fortunate arrangement in restraining Tahir when his precious sixteen dancers were whisked away in a mini bus to chalet accommodation at a nearby holiday camp, which had been necessarily commandeered at the last minute. He had wished to be with them and wanted to complain bitterly but his political awareness forced him to accept assurances that they would be well cared for and transported to all the functions on a daily basis. Nevertheless he was most unhappy with the arrangements despite it being his decision to include the dancers that had caused the problem

The dispirited Abberford group congregated in the main square just before lunch on Friday morning. The realisation that there was an influx of twinning guests from other countries was not universally welcomed on what they regarded as their special anniversary. Also, the weather was cool due to a low sea mist that enveloped the town. Unfavourable comparisons were made with previous visits and it was only when Antonio and Kathleen arrived to join them with their forecast of afternoon sunshine that spirits were lifted. By the time an early light lunch had been consumed their prophecy had proved correct and most of the group moved along to enjoy the promenade and beach facilities.

By eight o'clock they had gathered in the Town Hall foyer together with the other 150 invited guests and many of their hosts to be greeted by Hector Garcia.

Hector gave a very sincere welcoming speech to all, stressing that this was the occasion of the fiftieth anniversary of the link with their dear friends from England. He invited up to the stage and introduced Tahir Solanki and his wife and spoke generously of the role Antonio and Kathleen had played in forging such a long lasting and harmonious link between the towns.

The adjacent Great Hall was set with 300 places for what the Mayor had described as an extraordinary culinary experience, sampling only the very best dishes of the region and drinking the finest wines in the whole of Spain.

It was an impressive menu, including melon and *Iberico* ham and *chorizo* with fried black pudding and a main course of *Cochinillo Asado.*

The guests eagerly tucked into the meal with the exception of Tahir Solanki and his dance entourage.

"What's this?" demanded Tahir. The interpreter explained that it was the finest Spanish ham and spicy sausage, followed by a roast baby pig with a crisp fatty outside, perfect for those who liked pork rind. "Don't you know that Gujarati's are vegetarians?" asked Tahir in astonishment. "We cannot eat meat and we are not going to start now. What else is on the menu?"

Kathleen and Antonio were sitting close by and in the hope of defusing a potentially explosive situation, Antonio explained the unforeseen problem to the *Alkatea* and quickly suggested that they take the Gujarati's down the road to his sister's *tapas* bar. Hector apologised for the misunderstanding and personally escorted them to the bar. There, in the late evening sunshine, a large iron dish, full to the brim with the contents of an exquisite seafood *paella,* was busy bubbling on a hot plate. For the ravenous visitors it was very much to their taste and they eagerly accepted and consumed the generous helpings provided.

The following morning Tahir and his group, having made quite clear to Hector that in addition to being vegetarians, Gujaraties were also teetotal, gave their apologies for the vineyard visit and spent the day sightseeing around town. Not speaking the language they were generally bored and eventually returned to Hector's sisters tapas bar for a Spanish omelette and *gambas a la plancha*.

Neither were they football fans, showing no interest in the Spanish local derby and spent the evening ironing the creases out of their dance costumes.

A message the following morning from Hector reminded them that the afternoon event at the Arena was one of the outstanding culturally developed art forms in the whole of Spain and an event not to be missed. The Gujaratis lunched with Hector, Kathleen and Antonio once again at the safe haven of the *tapas* bar. After the meal Hector offered Tahir a large cigar, but was firmly admonished.

"I'm a doctor and know what damage smoking does to the human body. I have never smoked in my life and I would advise you to stop immediately if you want to live a long, healthy life."

Hector loved his cigars but reluctantly returned them to his jacket pocket before leading the party to the vast arena to witness the *corrida de toros*.

As they took their seats in the shade, the music began to play and Hector was, through Antonio as translator, at pains to explain how they were about to witness a classic cultural event on a par with the very best painting, music and dancing. Tahir had been enthralled by the excitement, music, colourful costumes and pageantry of the occasion. It only slowly dawned upon him that what he was witnessing was, in his opinion, a cruel blood sport; a cowardly sadistic tradition of slowly torturing a bull to death.

At the first sound of 'Ole' he rose from his seat, brushed past Hector and Antonio gesturing for the whole of his entourage to follow him from the arena. Never before, he was heard muttering, had he witnessed such cruelty to animals and any '*aficionado*' of such practices (as Hector had described himself) must be subhuman. How could these 'people' not know that representatives of the region where Mahatma Ghandi was born were naturally pacifists who regarded the whole *corrida* experience as barbaric and something left over from the Middle Ages. Gujaratis had no tolerance for this sort of behaviour.

Still recovering from the shock of the brutal *corrida,* Tahir ordered his dancers to practice for the following evenings festival. Hector was disappointed to note that the Gujaratis had failed to attend at the cultural visit to the Basque museum. Throughout the weekend all the other guests, despite initial language difficulties seemed to be enjoying themselves and he had received many compliments upon his programme and general organisational skills.

He took Antonio and Kathleen to one side.

"This was supposed to be a celebration of our long standing and successful friendship but the only people who do not seem to be enjoying it are your Mayor, his wife the Lady Mayoress, and his group. I have tried hard to please them but he does not like my excellent Spanish meats; he hates my Rioja wines some of which are the best in the world; he does not like football and speaks only of something called cricket; he tells me off for smoking and worst of all he insults me by leaving our beautiful *corrida* arena saying I am a cruel and sadistic man. Maybe it is that he is representing a left wing party and does not like or appreciate what our Basque Nationalist Party has done for this town or that he does not speak Basque or Spanish and does not understand our culture. I really don't know what it takes to please this man. Despite the heat, he always wears a suit and tie that is good for official occasions but not suitable for the daytime relaxed atmosphere of Iguderra. He must feel uncomfortable. Can you speak with him and put him on a friendly holiday footing before a Third World War breaks out? Find out what he likes before it is too late. Tomorrow is their last full day. If things don't improve before you go home everyone will have bad memories of the visit."

By mid afternoon, Antonio and Kathleen had tracked down Tahir Solanki and his wife to the dancers' holiday camp. There, they found the practice session in full swing and Tahir in relaxed mood. He and his wife were dressed in light, comfortable summer attire as they directed the dancers.

Antonio and Kathleen had no need to speak to Tahir. As they watched, they could see from his demeanour that he was happy. Eventually, he came over to them.

"Our routines are perfect," he enthused. "Tonight, at the festival when our traditional costumes will be worn, we will show Iguderra exactly what a culturally developed art form our dances are."

The evening started well. Tahir dressed in his impressive mayoral robe and chain of office. His wife wore a traditional, stylish long flowing sari. Hector and Alberto had arranged a comprehensive vegetarian meal for the whole group. At intervals during courses, demonstrations were given of the flamenco and fandango and everyone enjoyed the dramatic dances, colourful costumes and exciting sound of castanets.

After the final course, Hector announced that the Gujarati group would shortly take the floor to entertain with their traditional dances. The team left the Great Hall to change into their costumes, which had been carefully folded, and placed inside the black plastic refuse bags. They had taken them from the mini bus with the intention of leaving them in the changing rooms. When they saw that the flamenco dancers were temporarily occupying the rooms, they placed the bags in the corridor that led down towards the kitchen. Arriving back at the corridor, the bags were nowhere to be seen and a search of the changing rooms proved fruitless. Tahir's host, the Chief of Police was asked to investigate and ascertained that one of the kitchen staff, thinking they were bags of rubbish, had taken them outside in readiness for the Monday evening refuse collection. Half an hour previously, a refuse vehicle had arrived and taken all the waiting bags. The costumes were somewhere in the back of a refuse vehicle being transported to the tip.

On hearing the news, Tahir flew into a rage, considering the disappearance of the costumes as a personal sleight and an insult to his ancestry. He would not hear of the dancers continuing wearing just their normal western style jeans, tee shirts and casual tops. He demanded to know why the catering employee had been so stupid and argued fiercely with the head chef who vigorously defended his staff. Everyone could clearly hear heated voices behind the scenes and heads turned as the dispute, now involving all the dancers and catering staff, spilled out into the Great Hall.

There was much jostling, pushing and shoving. Accusations were shouted, intimidating threats made to the extent that some of the guests had to physically restrain the main protagonists from assaulting each other. Guests joined in the mêlée with the best intentions of preventing it getting out of hand but this only served to exacerbate the situation. Orders were shouted in several different languages but in the general uproar could not be heard or understood in the cacophony that raged all around. Tables were overturned, chairs knocked over and there were sounds of crashing crockery and breaking glasses as they fell to the floor. As a result of all this commotion, screams were heard as guests charged towards the exit. The physical impossibility of almost three hundred people trying to escape the rumpus in a disorderly fashion caused a logjam. It was an unedifying sight of people thrusting forward towards the door with many squashed and trapped in the middle unable to make progress. Attention turned towards self-preservation to the extent that the original cause of the fracas seemed to have been forgotten. The *Alkatea*, together with Antonio and Kathleen took refuge at the back of the Hall and could only watch despairingly as for several minutes, guests pushed and shoved like a gang of ruffians in an effort to break free.

Eventually the room cleared, leaving just Hector, Antonio and Kathleen to assess the damage. The room was strewn with hats and various items of clothing, overturned furniture, cutlery, tablecloths, napkins, and broken glass. The spilled red wine gave the room the appearance of a bloody battlefield. Suddenly realising the absurdity of it all, Kathleen broke out into uncontrolled laughter. Tears ran down her face as she tried to control herself. But it was no use and she couldn't stop, desperately trying to say in a fit of giggles, "At least nobody was injured or killed." Hector smiled ruefully, picked up a half open bottle of wine, found three unbroken glasses and filled them.

"Yes, we must at least drink to that," he said thankfully.

After Antonio and Kathleen had left, Hector stayed on to assess the damage. It was far worse than he had first thought. Many tables and chairs were broken, the main door damaged and the once beautifully polished floor stained and scuffed. Using his own building workforce, he arranged for the Great Hall to be cleared, cleaned and repaired at his expense. Tables, chairs and broken crockery were replaced using his firms bulk buying discount power with a local store. It was not his normal practice but he knew he would be held accountable for the damage that had occurred and wished to settle the matter without further fuss.

Tahir and his group had made a hasty retreat, hiring taxis to return to the holiday camp where they spent their final night. After what had happened Tahir did not want the embarrassment of having to stay with the Chief of Police. If it hadn't been for need of their passports, he would have found his way directly to the ferry port in Bilbao. In the event, he was spared what would have been an awkward moment by the Chief of Police's initiative in packing Tahir and his wife's belongings, including passports and handing them to Antonio, who with Kathleen was staying on for a few more days. Antonio was able to take them to the holiday camp where he insisted that as Mayor, Tahir must attend the farewell speech from Hector later that morning.

It was a subdued crowd that assembled inside the Town Hall. Several people limped into the building, others sported minor bruising and plasters covering small cuts but generally there was a feeling of guilt and shame about their behaviour the previous evening.
Hector did not wish to prolong their discomfiture but thanked them for coming adding that the dinner dance hadn't been quite the cultural occasion he had envisaged but it had turned out to be an unforgettable evening in more ways than one.
The mood was clearly one for getting away as soon as possible and Tahir, tail between his legs, thought better of giving a public response, merely shaking Hector by the hand and wishing him well for the remainder of his year in office. Both knew that they were unlikely ever to meet again and a short farewell suited their purpose.

It seemed a long journey home to Abberford but at least on the coaches without the sixteen costumes they were looking forward to additional space and comfort on the last leg of the journey home. Just after they set sail from Bilbao, the interpreter received a telephone call from the council's Chief Executive.

"What on earth has been going on? There are pictures all over the local morning paper of what looks like a gigantic rugby scrum and the press have already been on to me for a comment. Put the Mayor on the line, I can't hold them off much longer."

Tahir was quickly summoned and, being a past master of the perfumed response, glibly intoned down the line that there 'had been a little local difficulty but that things had been resolved and the twinning visit had been a great success'.

"I'll quote you on that," said the Chief Executive, "but I want you to come and see me as soon as you arrive back. An urgent problem has arisen."

The phone went dead leaving Tahir in suspense. The press were always distorting things but by the time he had prepared an official statement on the way back home, everything he thought would soon settle back to normal. He hadn't been brought up in a cricket loving world without fully mastering the art of *spin!*

The coach arrived at Abberford station on Wednesday afternoon. Tahir, now restored to his confident self, changed into his usual suit, shirt and tie, made his way quickly to the Chief Executives office and entered without knocking.

"Oh, it's you," barked the exasperated Chief Executive. "I've managed to get you off the hook with the press but we need to make a couple of decisions. I'm told that a problem had arisen about your expenditure of £1,600 on the council credit card. The interpreter telephoned me to ask for my approval of the payment but I have refused. Since I spoke with you this morning, Alberto Sanchez has been on the phone to say he has received a further bill for accommodation for your dancers, totalling £640.

I've got you out of trouble once but not a second time. I insist you pay all the additional costs from your own pocket. Alberto Sanchez told me the whole story of what happened. He said the loss of the costumes was not your fault but your subsequent behaviour, rightly or wrongly, aggravated the situation and it was only by chance that things did not get completely out of hand. Many people there had mobile phones and no doubt some of the photographs they took were forwarded to the press.

First thing next morning, Tahir walked swiftly into the Borough Treasurers office and placed his personal cheque for £2,240 and a sealed envelop upon the desk. "That will take care of everything. I'll leave you to tie up the loose ends," he said, quickly turning on his heel and leaving the room before the Treasurer had time to respond. The Treasurer's initial satisfaction upon seeing the cheque turned to frustration and anger when, upon opening the envelop he read the hand written note.

'Instruct the council's municipal insurance company to pay £2,400 for sixteen elaborate dance dresses at £150 each that were stolen during an official council function. When you have received the money, make out a cheque to me'.

Over the weekend, Hector Garcia had had second thoughts about his costly impromptu generosity. The Chief Engineer had inspected the work and had been delighted by the high-class finish. On Monday morning, he had contacted Hector to congratulate him and ask how much it had cost. Even after Hector had quickly added back the bulk discount sum, it came to less than the Council's estimate for similar work due to be carried out later in the year. Hector was told that if he would present his account it would be fully reimbursed.

Before Kathleen and Alberto left for Abberford, Hector invited them to his parlour to thank them for their fifty years support of the twinning arrangement. With deference to them for all they had achieved, he had decided to let bygones be bygones. Soon to be more than fully compensated by his council, he gave them a parting cheque for the attention of Tahir Solanky as a contribution towards replacement dance costumes.

Cassoulet of Castelnaudary

TIM'S SAUSAGES

The Mayor *(maire)* of Boise-en-Val, Gaston Thiebaut, sat down heavily in his kitchen chair. It was mid evening and he had just returned from Toulouse where he had attended a meeting for all newly inaugurated *maires*.

For him, the term 'newly inaugurated' was something of a misnomer, for he had just started his forty-third year as *maire*, having been elected for a further six years term for the eighth successive time. Once again, the term 'elected' was also a misnomer. The fact was that he had been returned unopposed on every occasion.

When his predecessor had retired after many years service, several of the older residents had been approached to take over the reins of office, but all had refused. They were from agricultural stock, having little interest in officialdom. Rules, regulations and paperwork were anathema to them.

So, as a last resort, the villagers had coerced a reluctant Gaston, a young man not too long out of school, to be their chosen representative. Heading the electoral list containing just the minimum number of candidates, his installation as the village's premier representative was automatic. He spent two days on an induction course and read books explaining the role of a *maire* but, as time past, his acquired knowledge of the job came from hands-on experience.

Over the years, he had learned of and spoken about the great democratic society in which we live, free speech, one man one vote, accountability to the electorate and acceptance that power was transferred peacefully from one political view to another. Once again however, the word 'political' was a misnomer, for he was not a member of any political party, had no firm political views and regarded politics with great suspicion.

He had attended important meetings in his time and witnessed very unsavoury behaviour from *maires* of one political persuasion or another - carping, backbiting, all sorts of skulduggery and wheeler dealing in efforts to demean each other. To him, this smacked of points scoring and practices verging upon corruption rather than democratic decision-making.

He had never made any contribution to such meetings. The great party machines gave little opportunity for a rural, independent *maire* to have a voice in proceedings and he had never asked to be allowed to speak, neither had he been called upon to do so.

Over the years, he had been greeted by excited, young newly elected *maires* and asked which town or village he represented. When he had replied Boise-en-Val, it was met by such puzzled responses as 'Boise what?' 'Boise where?' or *'Bon Courage!'* and that was the end of the conversation. If he had taken the time and trouble to explain where it was situated, it would not have been helpful or even remotely interesting to them as it was rarely visited, being very much off the beaten track. It's exact situation was 30 miles east of Toulouse in the foothills of the Black Mountains which stretched upwards towards the Pic du Nord at 3,500 feet, then down almost all the way to Beziers. One could buy a 1:20 Ordinance Survey map of the region and, after careful scrutiny, locate the name of the village, set in rolling hills, just off the D472.

The village had its origins as far back as the 11th century when it had grown into a thriving rural community, its fertile soil providing adequate feed for a miscellany of cattle. The village had sided with the Cathars at that time, but had been overrun by Catholic persecutors, the peasants slaughtered and the houses ransacked and burnt. There was little left of that era, save for a few artefacts that had been recovered following an archaeological 'dig' by students several years ago, who had unearthed what they considered to be the foundations of a medieval workshop. How the *maire* wondered, could they be so confident that a small pile of old stones, what he would have termed rubble, could be traced back to the Cathars? However, they were the 'experts', he had thanked them for their efforts and the pile of stones continued to remain in place, observed by no one.

The old church, with its faded date of 1528 above the main door, was the only remaining building from the distant past. After the second world war, the church regularly had congregations of fifty or more devout souls at its Sunday morning service. Now, it offered one short service on the last Sunday of each month. The current priest, a young, freshed-faced, jovial Sénégalese, regularly joked that once, his country had been progressively converted to Christianity by French missionaries, whereas now, he was the missionary attempting to convert the younger members of French society. Before his transfer overseas, he had preached to congregations of over five hundred people in his home town. Here in the South of France, he was responsible for sixteen rural churches and in Boise-en-Val, his average congregation totalled just five!

Today, many of the buildings scattered either side of the winding road which ran through the village, were now unoccupied. As recently as the nineteenth century, all these houses were home to families working on the land, but as the century turned and parents died, children migrated to larger towns such as Toulouse to obtain better paid jobs in the growing industries which were springing up all along the Garonne.

The present population could easily be counted. Fifty-two people occupying just twenty properties. Gaston knew them all from the oldest, Mrs Parmentier, who was cared for by her son and daughter-in-law, to the youngest, forty-eight year old Henri Vidal who, upon the death of his mother, had continued to work the land on the ten hectares attached to his house.

Gaston Thiebaut himself was a native of the village, naturally fluent in French and with a smattering of Occitan and Catalan, both of which his late parents, originally from Perpignan, had spoken. Gaston spoke with a distinctly unpolished French accent as though he had stones in his mouth, what the locals termed '*rocaille*'. He was a big man, not particularly tall at 5ft 7 ins, but wide and round. He led with his stomach, which he used as a battering ram to open doors and push his way forward between people in shops and crowded rooms. He was fond of the Catalan liking for bullfighting. With his dark hair, round lined face, set on top of his muscular shoulders without the appearance of any connecting neck, he gave the outward impression of the bull rather than the elegant matador. He was now a widower, his wife having died some years before. In his late sixties, he continued to produce and sell free range eggs on his plot of land to add to his small salary as *maire*. His body needed regular sustenance and he always prepared the easy options. Fried eggs and Toulouse sausage was his favourite, invariably washed down with one of the local wines, a *Malepere* or *Cabardes*.

On the anniversary of his eighth unopposed election as *maire*, he had tried to take stock of the village and his own circumstances. It was obvious to all that not only were his residents dying, but the village itself. When he had become *maire* those long forty-three years ago as a proud young man of twenty-six, the population had totalled two hundred and twenty-eight, as evidenced by the census of that year. Now, it had fallen to an all time low in his lifetime and if present trends were to continue, there would be no one left by the time of the next census.

Progress continued to be made in reviving Occitan. In major towns in the region, schools dedicated to the language had been established and the Occitan spelling was now included on street nameplates and town signposts. Yet, in his own village, there were no such signs, no school, doctor, dentist, library or even *salle polyvalente*. All these services were to be found in the next village of Jardin-en-Val, six miles to the south. Something must be done to rejuvenate Boise-en-Val, but what?

The only occupied official building of note was the Town Hall (*Mairie)*, where Gaston had his own office and where meetings took place. It comprised of six large rooms of which only two were now used. The imposing large wooden front door to which he had the key, had the word *'MAIRIE'* etched above the door in faded gold lettering. Inside was his own room with a leather topped desk, a small library of official books on the French *Republiques*, minutes of meetings held over the years and a cupboard containing a miscellany of official forms. The only recent addition was a photograph of the current French President affixed above the fireplace. The second room contained a large table surrounded by sixteen chairs, now more than sufficient to cater for the occasional meetings called as and when necessary.

One meeting, held annually, was a visit from the deputy director of the main Social Security office in Toulouse. It was the policy of Government to maintain and enhance the countryside. It regarded as vital the retention of villagers in their own homes by providing them with incentives to stay. Accordingly, although the farms and smallholdings were producing at below subsistence level, residents received support from Social Services to enable them to, as the 'National Plan of Objectives for the Enhancement of Rural Life' proudly boasted, 'enjoy a rewarding life in the beautiful rural setting which our French heritage has bestowed upon us'.

This support enabled the remaining residents to finance mobile phones as well as satellite dishes either on their roofs or in their gardens. All were avid supporters of Toulouse rugby XV and admirers of the flowing style of Catalan football giants, Barcelona. For most, watching television coverage of these games was the highlight of their lives.

This evening, one thing did however concern Gaston Thiebaut. When he had represented the village at countless functions and dinners, he was always being told that one village was famous for its make of cheese, another made the best wine in the whole of France, some village had just unveiled a statue to a famous military giant who had originated from there many years ago, or another had an art gallery in memory of their local hero whose water colours were acclaimed worldwide.
He could only listen; being unable to make a contribution, for Boise-en-Val had no such claim to fame. No artist, artisan, poet or soldier had merited adulation outside of the village. Come to think of it, Gaston could not recall anyone ever receiving recognition in Boise-en-Val, let alone the outside world. In fact, Boise-en-Val was one of the few or maybe the only village in France Gaston believed, that did not have a memorial to the two great wars as no one had given their lives in the struggles. In trying to redress this humiliating omission, it had been claimed that the three young boys from the family Ducrou, who fell in 1916, had links with the village. Their grandparents were thought to have lived in a cottage in Boise-en-Val, but this had long been disproved. The boy's names were inscribed on the official remembrance statue of a village further down the valley. No, Boise-en-Val had no claim to fame. It was dying and when dead, would just fade into history and not be missed.

The following week, Gaston's gloom for the survival of the village of his birth deepened further when 'young' Henri Vidal told him that he was moving to Toulouse to help in his sister and brother-in-law's catering business. His house would become vacant within weeks.
Now, when French property owners die, it is customary for their property to be passed on to their children. That is how the parents themselves came to acquire their properties - handed over from generation to generation.
As is common in France and particularly in Boise-en-Val, when a property is passed down to a family of several children who have married and moved on, it creates an argument amongst the inheritors, as the children cannot agree what to do.

'We can't sell it as we grew up there. It contains all of our childhood memories and is our heritage', they often claim. As a consequence, the property remains empty, falls into disrepair and becomes just a monument to life in bygone days. Such was the case in Boise-en-Val. Not a property had been sold for years and Gaston could not recall the last one. It was therefore a surprise when Henri Vidal informed him that he had asked a house agent to sell it, the sound reason being that his only sister and he agreed that the catering business could be profitably expanded if funds became available.

To the bewilderment and amusement of the neighbours, a sign soon went up on the gate of the property-

'*A VENDRE – MAISON ET 10 HECTARES EN BON ETAT*'

Autumn turned to winter, the biting *Tramontane* brought strong, cold winds to the valley and when the wind changed to *le Marin*, it precipitated several falls of heavy, moist white snow across the fields, which quickly turned to slush. Only the most necessary journeys were made during this time, the occasional lorry load of wood for the wide-open salon fires so beloved of the French, or the doctor to attend a sick patient. This was never a good time for prospective purchasers and Henri Vidal's house remained unoccupied and regarded by none. For one whole week, the '*A VENDRE*' sign had been totally obliterated by snow, but the odd person who had noticed it did not feel inclined to brush the snow away. What was the point?

After a very long winter, so common along the Black Mountain range, spring suddenly arrived. Technically, it was spring, but in reality, it was now mid May and to the locals, spring did not exist.

Gaston Thiebaut awoke one morning and parting his bedroom curtains, viewed with great satisfaction, a clear blue sky and the sun's bright rays burning off the early morning dew. He could see and hear the birds chirping. Yes, spring, or was it summer, had finally arrived.

During breakfast, which Gaston Thiebaut took adequate time to prepare, frying tomatoes and mushrooms then dropping two eggs into the hot fat, basting them until the yolks gained a thin film of white, his mobile phone rang. Gaston was not technically minded but was proud of being a mobile phone owner and kept it regularly on charge. As he rarely used it, he sometimes forgot where he had left it. This morning, breakfast was his top priority and by the time he had located the phone, the ring tone had ceased and the display screen informed him – one missed call. He could have established that it was the deputy director of Social Services calling to arrange his annual meeting and returned the call, but Gaston's attitude was that if someone wanted him badly enough, they would call back.

It wasn't the deputy director ringing back which disturbed Gaston's tranquil morning but a sharp rap on his front door brass knocker and a very loud voice enquiring with an urgent tone *"Monsieur le Maire, Monsieur le Maire?"*

He rose as quickly as he could, thinking that it must be some sort of emergency. The knocking continued until, opening the door he was confronted by a very large gentleman. He was so large that he dwarfed even the stocky figure of the *Maire*.

"Do I have the honour of addressing the *Maire* of Boise-en-Val?" beamed the gentleman, seizing Gaston's hand and giving it a mighty shake. Gaston was taken aback and could only nod feebly. His mind was racing wildly and thinking 'What does this fellow want with me'? He was flattered to be called '*Monsieur le Maire*' by a complete stranger and could not recall anyone ever being 'honoured' to make his acquaintance. When the stranger had released his hand, he stood to his full height to assess him. Even then, he was still some ten inches shorter and had to crane his short neck to look up and stare him in the face. The stranger was a veritable giant at 6ft 5ins and 18 stones. He stood there beaming, a large oval face, balding on top, but more than compensated by a generous moustache and beard. With his large girth, legs implanted firmly on the ground, he immediately reminded Gaston of a painting he had once seen of King Henry VIII of England.

The clock struck eleven and Gaston, reminded as all Frenchmen are at this hour, said "you're just in time for an aperitif."

He quickly invited this friendly stranger inside, took him through to the kitchen, pulled up two chairs and brought out a bottle of pastis and a carafe of iced water from his fridge. Whilst Gaston was pouring and providing a plate of olives coated in garlic, the stranger introduced himself as 'Tim Wilson from Lancashire, England'.

Gaston was even more puzzled. He had met the occasional English tourist, experiencing at first hand their lack of knowledge of the French language. He had listened in bewilderment as they had tried to converse with the odd words they thought they knew in the most appalling accent. Yet here, in Boise-en-Val, in his house, was a complete stranger, an Englishman, speaking fluent French with an accent which could be taken as that of an educated Parisian. Not only that, this young man seemed to have no difficulty in understanding Gaston's rough, rural accent that was often incomprehensible to some Frenchmen as well as most foreigners. Their glasses were emptied and quickly refilled, Gaston warming to this stranger. He introduced himself.

"Gaston Thiebaut, *Maire* of this village for forty-three years," he informed Tim.

Tim, a very hospitable person himself and full of bonhomie responded eagerly, "*Monsieur le Maire*", let me tell you straight away why I am here. I require your help in two very important matters."

This statement pleased Gaston. His very role as *maire* was to use all his years of experience to help people, although it was now rare for that help to be requested. "Although I am only in my early fifties," continued Tim. "I am university educated and spent twenty-five years in the Civil Service. I have worked in embassies in Paris and Bucharest, which helped me to become fluent in the French language and learn to enjoy and appreciate French culture. I took early retirement last year as it offered the freedom to explore a change of lifestyle. My wife and I have been on many holidays to France. She is a nursery school teacher and wishes to continue working for a few more years. We are looking for a property where we can take holidays several times a year and eventually settle in France on a permanent basis."

Gaston nodded, but was not aware of how he could help. "Yesterday *Monsieur le Maire*, I was in Mirepoix talking to estate agents. One agent advised me to consider looking at a vacant property in your village. He gave me your name and address and said that, as *Maire* of the village, you may be able to assist me,"

Gaston looked up in amazement. "You, you mean" he stuttered, "You mean Henri Vidal's old house? You mean you want to buy it? But no one has bought a house in this village for years."

He slowly gathered his thoughts, realising that what he had said in haste was not helpful to his old neighbour, Henri Vidal, so added "but then again, no other properties have been for sale and I'm told that Henri's is very desirable."

Tim continued, "I drove over this morning and have just seen the property from the outside. The grounds are just what I am looking for, but it looks like the house will need some serious renovation. Before I consider it, I need to speak to you about my plans."

In France, the *Maire* has a number of decision-making powers to enable him to organise life in the best interests of the inhabitants. Gaston listened patiently whilst Tim explained his proposals.

"*Monsieur le Maire*," said Tim, rising to his full imposing height and standing above the puzzled Gaston, "I believe that I need your permission after I have brought my caravan across from England to live in it in the grounds of the property whilst repairs are carried out. It is a modern, fully equipped caravan, but there are no camping sites around here and the most convenient location would be in one of the paddocks within the grounds. It may be that it would look out of character in this village, but it would only be for a relatively short time."

Gaston rose slowly to his feet, put both his arms behind his back, which made his stomach protrude even further and started pacing the kitchen. To give himself time to think, he said in a low, slow thoughtful voice, "Permission for a caravan within the grounds eh? This is not a matter that can be taken lightly. Permissions can be given but consultations will be necessary with the neighbours. There will be forms to complete, oh so many forms in France," adding, "France has a great administrative history and reputation you understand and this must be respected."

"Sir," responded Tim, "Let me have the forms and I will complete them now to save time."

"Ah," exclaimed Gaston, not wishing to be rushed. He did have appropriate forms filed away somewhere in the *Mairie*, but knew he could not locate them without an extensive search. He still wished however to help Henri Vidal but wanted to get to know Tim Wilson a little better. The clock on the mantelpiece struck noon and despite his large breakfast, the aperitif had revived his appetite and for him as for all rural Frenchmen, midi meant lunch.

"Let us consider this together in a civilised way," he declared "and what could be more civilised than lunch and a bottle of wine?" Tim sat down as Gaston reached to open the fridge door and took out a number of roundels of his favourite Toulouse sausage and two large pork chops. Into the frying pan they went, together with tomatoes and seasoning. Ten minutes later, all was ready. A large baguette had been sliced and a good red wine from Gaston's personal cellar, uncorked. The feast was served with a helping of Dijon mustard.

"Yes, these permissions are a tricky business," muttered Gaston "one must not be seen to be setting a precedent." Tim wondered what 'precedent' Gaston thought he would be setting if he could not remember the last time a house sale had been made, but realised that his request had been put and was now in the *maire's* hands. He must bide his time.

At the end of the meal, Gaston prepared an expresso for them. As they consumed the thick, black liquid into which Gaston had stirred three sugar lumps, he sat forward, looking towards Tim.

"*Monsieur Wilson*," he said, "I have given your request a great deal of thought and considered it from every angle. Taking everything into account, I have concluded that I am unable to give you written permission."

Tim's face dropped. Surely his was a simple demand that would help a former neighbour and breath new life into the village. What objection could Gaston possibly have?

Continued Gaston, "I cannot give you written permission because none is needed. No, you have only asked to live in your caravan temporarily and to my knowledge, not being a permanent feature, it requires no permission. It is part of the necessary equipment for what is termed 'work in progress' so is exempt from such permissions. Yes indeed, exempt."

He thumped his fist on the table like a judge banging his gavel to restore order in court.

It hadn't been the caravan that had concerned Gaston, but the thought of locating and attempting to complete all those complicated forms which would have had to be sent to Toulouse for approval. It didn't bear thinking about and something that he considered should be avoided at all costs. The annual tax forms were bad enough without compounding the problems. His solution neatly sidestepped the administrative nightmares and provided an instant way forward. He considered his role to be that of helping progress, not hindering it. The fact that it would save him an enormous amount of time and anxiety was but a minor consideration. Tim's face broke into a huge beam. He was used to people making sensible decisions and Gaston, despite the horrors he had heard of French bureaucracy, had not disappointed him. He reached across and for the second time that day, shook the *maire's* hand forcibly.

As Gaston cleared the table, he noticed that Tim, whom Gaston had thought to be a gourmet, had eaten everything except the Toulouse sausage. So as not to offend this interesting Englishman and not wishing to place any obstacles in the way of the sale of Henri Vidal's house, he remained silent about it.

"You did say there were two things I could help you with," said Gaston, looking across at Tim, "what is the other?"

"*Monsieur le Maire*, one step at a time, I am returning to Mirepoix and will come back to view the house tomorrow now that you have set my mind at rest about the caravan. The other matter can wait until later."

Tim did indeed return next day, called briefly on the *maire* to thank him for his help and returned to England. Gaston heard no more until a month later Tim returned with his wife Brenda. In the early afternoon, they tracked down Gaston to his office in the *Mairie* where he had just finished his annual meeting with the deputy director of Social Services from Toulouse. His meeting had been nothing special to report, no new funds or initiatives had been offered and the deputy director had not spent much time in what he had called this 'terminally ill' village.

Gaston's gloom was immediately lifted when Tim introduced him to Brenda, adding that she had liked the situation of Henri Vidal's house, if not the house itself. Following the long, hard winter months without any potential buyers, the agent had discussed matters with Henri. Henri reluctantly agreed to accept from Tim and Brenda a much reduced offer, sweetened somewhat by the fact that they had no outstanding mortgage, were not in a chain to sell and could pay the full amount in cash.

Gaston was delighted for two reasons. First of all, the population of the village would increase overall by one. Secondly, as Tim was fifty-one and Brenda only forty-four, she would not only be the youngest member of the community (albeit part-time at the start) but they would reduce the average age of the village by almost a full year. He would be able to report this to the unfeeling deputy director in due course. Naturally, a glass of wine was offered to the couple and appropriate congratulations conveyed.

By mid-summer after Tim and Brenda had completed the sale the *'VENDU'* notice was removed by the agent. They had driven down from England with their caravan in tow and installed it in the small paddock about twenty yards from the house. Tim then set out to organise the renovation work. He employed an architect to draw up plans and obtained quotations from builders for the main alterations. He took on the task of converting one of the outbuildings himself.

Brenda returned to work in England early in September. Tim remained to continue work on the outbuilding and supervise the house improvements, the architect's plans having been finally passed with only a few minor amendments.

Tim and Brenda had made an arrangement with the *maire* that once a week, whilst they were in the caravan, that they would cook an evening meal that they could easily carry over to Gaston's house a short distance away. The caravan was too small for all of them whereas Gaston's house had a large kitchen with the kind of rustic table and chairs so admired by the English. Being a widower, Gaston always welcomed company, especially company bearing food. Food was one of his chief enjoyments of life and this arrangement saved him from the arduous task of cooking. He came to appreciate that both Tim and Brenda were excellent cooks, using all the local produce to prepare tasty, enjoyable meals. They also enjoyed their food and naturally, the South-West France wines.

It was the following March, when Tim returned from a few weeks back in England, that Gaston discovered the second important matter upon which Tim required his help.

Whilst work had recommenced on the house after the winter cold, Tim continued to live in the caravan. He had arranged that one evening, he would prepare a meal to carry across to Gaston's house.

Gaston had prepared the table. He uncorked the wine, watching Tim serve the food. Tim had prepared a mixed grill of succulent lamb and pork chops, slices of beef, black pudding and sausages, together with a delicious array of local vegetables-tomatoes, carrots and mushrooms, accompanied by a jug of onion gravy, with a hint of garlic. The smells were mouth-watering and Gaston could hardly wait to start. Large helpings were served and the meal commenced. It wasn't long before Tim had cleared his plate and Gaston had devoured everything except the sausages, which he thought looked somewhat pale, thin and uninteresting. He had taken one bite. It was difficult to pinpoint exactly as to why he did not enjoy it, but the taste was not to his liking. The sausage did not, in his opinion, cut very precisely; seeming to explode all over the plate. It contained what tasted like bread and a large amount of fat. Where was the meat he had thought?

Gaston nevertheless thanked Tim. "That was excellent Tim, but the err, err, …" "Sausages," interrupted Tim. "You don't like my sausages eh Gaston?"

"Where did you get them from?" asked Gaston, ignoring the question. "Made them myself from a special recipe," responded Tim, "and as you mention it, that is the second thing you can help me with."

He went on to explain that since retirement, he had been looking for a business venture and was sure he had stumbled across one.

"When Brenda and I have been on holiday in France in our caravan," he explained, "we have bought foodstuffs from many a travelling shop - vegetables, bread, cakes, meats - anything we have needed which a vendor sells. Several times in areas like the Dordogne and Provence, we have seen butchers selling produce made in England. We have observed crowds of English people, residents and holidaymakers alike, flock to buy from them. The one item that sells above all others is the English sausage. It has attained legendary status. We have done some research and found that there is a large English resident population in this area from Toulouse to Beziers, but no English butcher to serve them with what they like. There are some English shops and the occasional travelling butcher, but that does not satisfy demand. What is needed is someone who can make and supply English sausages on a regular basis. I have, as you have seen, been hard at work converting one of the outhouses of our property with the intention of making and selling English sausages. I need health certification which I have already applied for, but also need to obtain permission to sell at local markets and fairs such as Mirepoix, Ceret, Quillan, Esperaza and Olonzac. This is where you could assist me in contacting the local *maires* and sponsoring my applications."

Gaston looked at him in astonishment, thinking he had taken leave of his senses.

Pouring him another glass of wine, he sat back in his chair, thinking about what Tim had asked him to do.

"Let me be clear about what you said," he spluttered. "You want to make and sell English sausages, sell English sausages here in France, in the South-West of France, where we have Toulouse sausages, the finest in the world? Is that what you are saying, because if so, it doesn't make sense? No self-respecting Frenchman would touch them. They are so full of fat and contain so little meat. It's madness. You will be wasting your time and will lose all your money. Don't do it or even consider it," he implored.

"You must understand," he continued, "that this region is famous for *cassoulet,* one of the greatest dishes that French regional cooking has produced. Hidden beneath a layer of creamy golden haricot beans are a combination of smoked bacon, a couple of pigs feet, half a duck, chunks of pork rind and the *coup de grâce,* a number of delicious garlicky pork sausages. With such an abundance of these local ingredients, your English sausage just pales into insignificance."

Undeterred, Tim clapped him on the back in a friendly manner.

"Gaston, its all a matter of taste. I know that you saw I did not finish the Toulouse sausage you cooked for me last year. I found it too meaty. Today, you have left the English sausage I prepared for our meal. Many English people have told me that they cannot eat *merguez* or *andouillette* sausages either. They are not used to them, find them too spicy or do not like the texture. In their own way, all these sausages are excellent, its just that the French prefer their Toulouse and other types of sausage and the English have been accustomed to their own. Believe me Gaston; I would not even consider this business if I did not think it would become successful."

"Of course I will help in any way I can, but I will bear no responsibility when you go bankrupt," replied Gaston.

He was as good as his word in helping Tim obtain market licences for the sale of his sausages. He talked to the *maires* explaining as well as he could the situation. The general view was that this Englishman's idea was extremely foolish but if he had money to throw away, as long as he paid the market rent, then so be it.

"I've advised him the best I can but he just will not listen," said Gaston. "He is a friendly fellow and says he is confident he will succeed. The only way to find out is to let him try so I should be grateful for your help in obtaining a licence for him at your market."

The first week in April saw Tim drive his vehicle with a refrigeration unit in the back full of newly made English sausages to his first market in Olonzac. Tim set up his stall. Sporting a Union Jack waistcoat, a white straw hat and looking all the world like a modern day King Henry VIII, Tim rang a hand bell, shouting "roll up, roll up, buy your best English sausages, seven different flavours," at the top of his voice.

He had paid rent from 9.00 to 17.00 but such was the success of his sales, that he had sold his entire stock by mid afternoon. No only did English people buy them but he was soon enticing curious French people to his stall. He had cooked several samples of each type of sausage. After their first free offering, they immediately placed an order. He had to close his stall early, promising to return with more stock on his next visit.

Gaston saw Tim arrive back in Boise-en-Val much earlier than expected and feared the worst for him.

"I'm sorry my friend," he commiserated, "I knew those sausages of yours would not find many takers, being too fatty by half. France is a country steeped in tradition when it comes to food. No, it's Toulouse sausages or nothing in this part of the world. I hope you are not too disappointed and you have not lost too much money."

Tim laughed. "Gaston, you didn't believe me when I said it was a matter of taste. The customer is always right. If you know what they want and can supply it, they will buy. It's simple supply and demand economics. That's what happened today. English people and many French too had a taste of what they liked and *voila* - everything was sold by 15.00."

Gaston, recognising a cause for celebration, brought out two glasses and a bottle of blanquette de Limoux. "I have to hand it to you Tim. My friends and I would never have believed it, but you have proved us all wrong. Here's to your continued success. *Sante,*" he said raising his glass and clinking it against Tim's.

This was just the start of Tim's enterprise. He found himself over the next few months increasing his output in response to demand. His business expanded to the point where he was able to arrange for other market traders to sell his sausages at markets which he did not have time to attend.

Despite his early misgivings, Gaston revelled in Tim's success. The local *maires* in the areas where Tim or his representatives stood the market were equally astonished by the English sausage sales. They were becoming famous throughout the region. When next Gaston telephoned the deputy director of Social Services, he was able to inform him proudly that he had reversed the trend of decline in Boise-en-Val and the population was now increasing. "Younger people are looking to move in here," he declared, "and I see educated, overseas people with savings as the future for us, mark my word."

Before the next regional conference of *maires*, Gaston wrote to the chairman, saying that after forty-three years of attending such events and never having been called to speak, he would be grateful for an opportunity this time as he had important things to say. The chairman could think of no reason after such a long period of inactivity why Gaston should not be called. He agreed to his request without any expectation that he would say anything remotely interesting. But, forty-three years was a long time to wait and he deserved a chance. As chairman, he also had the authority to cut short his speech if delegates became restless. He had to consult the 1:20 map to locate Boise-en-Val and he paged through the Municipal Journal containing a summary of each town and village's statistics and history. He noted that the only two entries for Boise-en-Val were its extremely low population and absence of any community debt, neither of which surprised him at all. No industry, no famous sons or daughters, no buildings of note, nothing. The village had just been left to go to rack and ruin.

The conference was held in the *Capitole*, Toulouse, attended by over five hundred local *maires*. There were three speakers before Gaston; a former Deputy Prime Minister, a leading industrialist and a member of the European Commission. All made confident speeches, imparting their particular knowledge and advising how best it could be used to the benefit of the region. After such professional presentations from skilled orators, the chairman wondered what he had let himself in for when he announced "and our next speaker will be *Monsieur* Gaston Thiebaut, for forty-three years, *maire* of Boise-en-Val."

Gaston rose to his feet and after smoothing his tricolour sash, walked slowly down the central isle, climbed the four steps to the stage and took his place at the rostrum. The chairman became even more apprehensive when he observed that Gaston appeared to have no notes.

He started by reminding the assembled *maires* that he had listened over the years to the successes of the towns and villages of his colleagues. Yes indeed, Castres had erected a statue in memory of *Jean Jaures.* Albi had the *Toulouse Lautrec* museum and art gallery. Carcassonne had *La Cité,* Castelnaudary was renowned for its *cassoulet* and there were many other examples. Sadly, he had never been able to promote the declining village of Boise-en-Val.

"This year however *Monsieur* Chairman," he announced proudly, throwing his shoulders back and making his stomach protrude as if deliberately pointing to delegates in the audience, "things have taken a turn for the better. For some years," he continued seriously "we have been developing our rural development strategy in Boise-en-Val. Now, after all our hard work, the strategy is paying off, reversing the decline in rural population and bringing jobs into the community. We assessed our position and promoted Boise-en-Val in the international market as an ideal place to invest and set down roots. We have been successful in attracting foreign investment both in housing and job creation. *Monsieur* Chairman, fellow *Maires*," he concluded, "All of us must look to the future and be prepared to adapt, seek imaginative new ways to enhance our prosperity. We have done that in the most entrepreneurial way and we know it works."

He returned to his seat to loud, prolonged and appreciative applause. The chairman was not just relieved, but most impressed. He had just heard a local, rural *maire* speaking without notes make a bigger impact on the delegates than the three professionals who had preceded him. He thanked Gaston for his 'most illuminating and wide ranging speech'. He was not too concerned that Gaston had carefully avoided mentioning the extent of what he meant by population increase, international market, foreign investment or the nature of the jobs created. Gaston had always followed the advice of his father, who had once told him when making a speech to 'stand up, speak up and shut up'. This is what Gaston had done to perfection and he had captured the mood of the conference. His speech was good on rhetoric if a little short on detail, but it was certainly his day. During the break for lunch, Gaston was besieged by delegates wishing to know more and even the European Commissioner congratulated him and gave him his telephone number.

"Give me a call next week at my Brussels office," he had said.

In the afternoon, the conference voted on 'Election of Officers for the following year'. When it came to nominations for membership of the 'Rural Community Development Committee', Gaston was proposed and seconded by two *maires* from market centres where Tim was successfully selling his sausages. Word was spreading.

After the conference, each committee held a brief meeting to vote for the election of Chairman and agree the date and venue of the first meeting of the year.

"After that wonderful speech of yours Gaston Thiebaut, I think you are just the person we are looking for," said one member. This was immediately seconded and Gaston was the unanimous selection of all. Taking the chair to arrange the first meeting, Gaston quickly counted the number of committee members. There were sixteen in total.

"Ladies and Gentlemen," he announced, "the first meeting of the year will be held in Boise-en-Val." Again, it was unanimously thought as a nice touch for the Chairman to host a meeting in his own village. Especially as it was a village they had never been to before and in most cases, never heard of.

Gaston's speech had convinced them that they had to look to the future, examine alternative approaches, discover different avenues and places, including Boise-en-Val.

So, on the first Tuesday in July, after carefully consulting the Ordinance Survey 1:20 map then inserting 'Boise-en-Val' into their satellite navigation systems, sixteen members prepared to drive to the village.

Allowing adequate time to arrive by noon, they found their way onto the D472. At the village boundary they were greeted by the large sign Gaston had erected, financed by a grant received following his telephone call to Brussels.

WELCOME TO BOISE-EN-VAL

HOME OF TIM'S SAUSAGES

The Birthday cake of Marie-France Delfort

THE VIAGER

Nestled in the hills twenty kilometres above the fashionable town of Nice lay the charming village of Lodiza, home to Marie-France Delfort. An only child born to impoverished parents living in a small terraced cottage on the outskirts of the village she had left school at twelve years of age and been sent to work in service to earn much needed money. From humble beginnings she could look back on a life of privilege and some luxury but one that had seen her fortunes fluctuate almost to the point of despair.

Developing into an attractive lively girl, she had had no shortage of boyfriends. Small, slim, with short jet black hair that enhanced her high cheekbones, she exuded that classic French chic that immediately caught the attention of all the local boys, several of whom had asked her to marry. Despite lack of formal education she was sufficiently astute as to bide her time and play the field. Before long she caught the eye of Joel, son of a wealthy local butcher.

Joel had served his time in the trade and been groomed to continue the long line as head of the family business. In his mid twenties, Joel soon proposed to Marie-France and they were quickly married, living with his parents in the family home, 4, *rue Pied du Renard*. It was a large *'maison de maitre'* situated in extensive grounds in the heart of the village, an imposing house built of local stone with seven bedrooms, an elegant staircase, wide corridors with parquet flooring and high ornamental ceilings. When the heavy wooden shutters were drawn back, sunlight streamed through the large windows giving the house a delightful luminosity.

Their two sons were born in successive years before her twenty-first birthday. Marie-France had cared lovingly for them and with domestic assistance had tended to their every need. The butchers was a successful business established as long ago as 1826, now with lucrative contracts to supply local schools. Marie-France had no need to work, occasionally assisting in the shop when necessary. She became a stalwart of the local community, reliable, dependable and a friend to all who knew her. They were a rich family and became renowned for their regular *soirées* at 4, *rue Pied du Renard*. Joel ensured that Marie-France received the best of everything. They regularly shopped at the Nice boutiques, ate in stylish restaurants and indulged their passion for gambling at the casino or Cagnes-sur-Mer racecourse.

The two sons married and over time presented Marie-France with five grandchildren. Ten great-grandchildren followed. Throughout his working life, Joel was both industrious and generous. As business blossomed, the couple's social lifestyle became hectic if somewhat flamboyant and extravagant. Upon Joel's retirement the eldest son continued as head of the family business. It was of great consolation to Marie-France that, when Joel died following a brief illness the long standing family firm continued to bear the name Delfort.

A cheerful and optimistic person she could always be relied upon to look on the bright side, counting her blessings that she had enjoyed good health and fortune throughout most of her life. She continued to live at 4, *rue Pied du Renard*, her sons and families who lived nearby, on hand to help and keep a watchful eye upon her.

Not long after Joel died, the local council, in an attempt to boost trade and revitalise the village succumbed to pressure, allowing construction of a shopping precinct and affordable housing on the edge of the village. A national supermarket chain became the anchor development and started to sell everything the local shops sold at vastly discounted prices. Over the next three years, business at Marie-France's son's butchers declined and long held contracts lost to such an extent that it was no longer profitable. Cost cutting measures were implemented and staff reduced but losses mounted. Attempts were made to sell it as a going concern but to no avail. The family business of 150 years standing closed, the shop cleared of fixtures and fittings and left empty to deteriorate.

The once thriving business that had provided continuous income for a very comfortable standard of living was now gone and future expectations of prosperity dashed. The elder of Marie-France's sons was out of work and the other had lost the inheritance he had taken as his birthright.

The unemployed son tried his utmost to secure a steady job but all he could find was irregular low paid employment - seasonal harvesting and odd jobs for grateful but unreliable neighbours. Lodeza still continued to attract holiday visitors but the heart of the former prosperous business area had been decimated by cheaper out of town outlets.

Marie-France tried her best to ease their burden, growing vegetables for them from her spacious garden, even helping with expenses when one of her grandchildren married. But she was unable to shake off her habits of a lifetime and found she had little to spare.

After Joel's death, Marie-France retained the services of her domestic help and chauffeur/gardener. She did not wish her lifestyle to change and continued to indulge in shopping sprees and frequent visits to both casino and racecourse. Welcomed with open arms at all these establishments as a regular and valued customer, she was on first name terms with management and regarded as a virtual member of their families. She regularly received complimentary meals in the racecourse restaurant and free initial bets in the casino.

Few, including Marie-France herself realised the full extent of her profligacy until one evening at the racecourse following a profitable start, she placed all her winnings on the hot favourite of five runners in the last race. Entering the bar to order a final drink and view the race as the runners rounded the first bend, she only counted four horses racing by and was dismayed to see her chosen mount some distance away tamely cantering back to the paddock. She went to the PMU betting office to recover her substantial stake money but was informed that as the horse had come under starter's orders and had failed to run, her bet was not reimbursable. Such was the amount that she marched down to the enclosure and demanded to speak with a steward. The apologetic fellow told her that the rules of racing applied and that no refund would be forthcoming. She asked to see the medical officer's certificate that the horse was unfit to run but with a shrug of his shoulders, the senior steward said that the horse had suffered from a 'headache'. All bets were the entitlement of the PMU and regrettably there was nothing he or she could do about it. Her large wager was lost.

Several days later, she received a letter from her bank manager demanding that she call to see him urgently. At the meeting, he stressed that little remained of her former investments and savings and that at her current rate of spending she would be destitute within the year.

Marie-France loved her house that held so many happy memories but regretfully decided the only way she could help herself and her sons was to sell and move to a smaller place or even a warden controlled retirement flat. It was the last thing she wished to do but it seemed the only solution. Reluctantly, without informing her family, she instructed a house agent to value her property and place it on the market.

4, *rue Pied du Renard* was an elegant property that Marie-France and her family had maintained to a high standard. It was the most desirable one in the area and the agent was confident that despite his very considerable valuation it would attract a discerning buyer if not locally, from the national or international market.

When the family became aware of Marie-France's action, they were most supportive. If the truth were known, that very proposal had been a topic of conversation between them for some time but none had been bold enough to raise it with Marie-France for fear of offending her. To a man, they were enthusiastic to the point of consulting the papers each day in search of a suitable small property for her. Over the following months, several possibilities became available but subject to sale of the *'maison de maitre'* no firm commitment could be made. The agent acting for Marie-France regularly reported interest in her property and from time to time arranged to show potential buyers its benefits as a prestigious place to live. As is often the case with such properties, it was too large for most and too expensive for the rest. One or two what the agent disdainfully referred to as 'silly offers' were received and the house remained unsold.

It was at this juncture that M. Rene Finot arrived on the scene. M. Finot was a Parisian of some standing. In his modest opinion, there were few more important people than he. He introduced himself as a man of substance achieved as a financial consultant in the city. He was a shrewd operator always on the lookout for a financial opportunity, no matter how small that he could invest in, nurture and eventually sell at a nice profit - thank you very much!

At 46 years of age, Rene Finot was looking to expand his property empire of several luxury apartments in the most desirable *arrondissements* of Paris that he let at what many would consider to be extortionate rents. He knew the property market inside out and aimed his lettings at tenants who wished to live at fashionable addresses no matter what the cost. There never seemed to be a shortage of such people willing and able to meet his rentals and consequently M. Finot's reputation as well as his bank balance flourished.

He considered that at this stage of his life he should be looking forward to a little relaxation for his family and himself. His attention had been drawn to a small but succinct advertisement in the property section of *Paris Match* –

> **'For sale, an elegant 'maison de maitre' set in the**
> **tranquil countryside close to the iconic town of Nice.**
> **Live like a Lord of the Manor and profit from**
> **an elegant property with investment potential'.**

Rene had liked what he had read, particularly the phrases 'Live like a Lord' and especially 'investment potential'. A site visit appeared to be essential and one was duly arranged with the agent for the following week. Marie-France was primed to ensure that the house and garden were in pristine condition and told to be available to provided M.Finot and his family with details of the benefits of living in such a fine property surrounded by beautiful countryside.

The imposing residence impressed the entire Finot family, Rene himself, his wife Justine, their two married daughters and husbands. Although Rene Finot was his own man it was fair to say that the decision to buy was both instantaneous and unanimous. Following a long conversation with Marie-France, Rene Finot took his leave and beckoned the estate agent to join him for a private conversation in the main lounge.

The agent was fully prepared for tough negotiations on the price. He had observed M. Finot's manner and whilst not at all liking this self-important individual, put aside all personal feelings for what was purely a business transaction. He was used to bartering and would obtain the best price for his client and as much commission as he could for himself. It wasn't everyday in such a small community that a prime property came onto the market and he was keen to make the most of his opportunity.

After a short bout of friendly sparring, M.Finot came abruptly to the point. In his opinion, there were several matters the agent had overlooked or had deliberately concealed. He was a Parisian and used to Paris standards. The property was certainly spacious and appealing but he pointed to its age, the slight dampness he had observed in the downstairs rooms compounded by the old fashioned décor. There was no central heating or air conditioning. The house did not seem to have been recently re-wired and amazingly for grounds of such dimension, they lacked a swimming pool, tennis court and even a basic sprinkler system. The only two things that rivalled Paris were the asking price and land tax.

The agent listened closely without comment to this overbearing man until finally the rasping voice concluded its tirade with a take it or leave it offer of just half the advertised price. He politely countered (untruthfully) that a somewhat higher bid had already been rejected at which point M.Finot announced that his price would be available for one week only following which his interest would terminate.

On their way home, the family found Rene Finot in cheerful mood despite lack of agreement to purchase. Everyone had been impressed by the house, loved the area but were disappointed that nothing had been concluded. Rene Finot was rich and the asking price a mere fraction of his wealth. They knew that despite his riches he was never disposed to pay more than what he considered something to be worth (even to the extent of occasionally purchasing clothes that he liked from retro shops) but they were surprised by his sunny demeanour when seemingly thwarted to land a prize he had so obviously coveted.

Rene Finot had however done some homework. During his conversation with Marie-France, he had asked her many questions and observed her closely. She had told him that she was 78 years of age, had lived in the house since she married 59 years ago and was forced to sell to financially aid her family. She wasn't getting any younger and found managing such a large house an increasing burden. He was informed that she was concerned about the failure of the butchery business and of the apparent lack of future prosperity for the family that caused her to have sleepless nights. She was also worried about moving from her home and wondered what the future held for her. Rene Finot had listened and expressed sympathy but inwardly he felt that her problem was more to do with inheritance than anything else. It was one thing to build a successful career from scratch as he had done and another for a family member to take over a flourishing business based on the endeavours of others. He wondered why when it was obvious that times and business practice were constantly changing that the eldest son had not anticipated this and tried something different rather than sit back and watch his butchery empire slide into oblivion. The village population had increased but that did not necessarily mean that they would automatically support local business. Customers had become much more discerning and demanded choice and most of all, value. The son, he thought, must have a typical country villager mentality of expecting the good times to continue forever, a stay at home *'casanier'* unwilling to look beyond the end of his nose and incapable of thinking that there was a big broad world outside ready and waiting for innovators. The price he had offered was fair based upon all the circumstances. He certainly did not regard himself as an eager benefactor to the extent that he would underwrite their financial future by paying the asking price. No, Rene Finot was thinking of pursuing a much more speculative strategy.

Upon his return to Paris he immediately contacted a colleague, an actuarial consultant to a number of leading insurance companies and pension funds. Rene Finot was soon to know that the average life expectancy for women in Lodiza and district was 82 years and 328 days. Marie-France Delfort was past her 78th birthday and there was no history of longevity in her family. Her mother had died aged 79 and her father very suddenly at only 68. The objective of Rene Finot's interest in such matters was to further his knowledge of the *Viager.*

The *Viager* he knew was an accepted and occasionally used system approved by the French government as a means of reducing dependence on social security programmes for the elderly. It operated through a contract drawn up by a lawyer between two willing parties whereby an elderly person would benefit from sale of their home whilst retaining lifetime use. For both parties it was a high risk gamble based upon how long the seller would likely live. For many, such an arrangement would be regarded as unseemly but to a risk taker such as Rene Finot it was merely a business transaction and in his view, a good one for him.

From the information he had gleaned, M. Finot could sense a quick killing (not that he would be instrumental in Marie-France's sudden departure) in that the statistics would prove to be correct and that Marie-France would die before or around her 84th birthday. It seemed a situation ready made for a man of M. Finot's calibre. At 46 years of age, such an arrangement could see him become the owner of this property at a knock down price sooner rather than later.

The agent received M. Finot's suggestion of a *Viager* and after consulting French law on the subject and the likely commission he would stand to receive, telephoned Marie-France to say that it might be just the sort of deal that would be of interest to her. He outlined the system of operation involving receipt by her of a lump sum payment, an inflation proof monthly sum, with the buyer meeting repair and maintenance costs, fees, commission and the annual land tax. To an inveterate gambler such as Marie-France it seemed too good to be true. Short of funds, she was now being offered money with which she could help her family and the chance to remain in 4, *rue Pied du Renard*. With a guaranteed life annuity that also qualified for generous tax relief she could continue as before (perhaps sometimes applying the break, but only occasionally). And so what if she did die? Her sons would have benefited from the windfall (much less than they would have expected certainly but beggars can't be choosers) and in any event the sudden emergence of a solution to her problems had made her feel at ease, more confident and optimistic than for many a year.

Her agent was pleased to inform Rene Finot of his client's interest in a *Viager* and a lawyer was appointed to oversee the agreement. Rene Finot flew down to Nice and met with Marie -France before the fine details were calculated. He wanted one final check to confirm his original judgement. He had heard of elderly people feigning illness, even applying make-up to appear ill with the intention of fooling buyers. Some tried to falsify their date of birth especially those born overseas where records were unreliable. But no, Marie-France appeared to be an honest, respectable woman and he was content to rely upon the accuracy of the data presented to him.

A free market value was made of the property. This was promptly halved and in accordance with Marie-France's age, the lump sum (known as the *bouquet*) was set at 30% of the lower figure. Marie-France's age was taken to find the set percentage relating to the calculation of the monthly payment to arrive at the sum due. To Rene Finot, such sums were trifling amounts but his big prize would be when he took possession of this *'maison de maitre'*. His Lord of the Manor status beckoned. He had been lucky in life and his good fortune was not going to stop now.

The lawyer drew up the papers, both parties signed and the *bouquet* paid to Marie-France. This was temporarily placed on deposit until the family had agreed a settlement between themselves. The terms of the *Viager* were examined. It stated that Marie-France would be able to remain in her home for the rest of her life but did not preclude anyone else living with her.

An amicable solution was found whereby the elder son and his family would move in to look after Marie-France, for him to receive a third of the *'bouquet'* and prepare their house for holiday lettings. The other two-thirds *'bouquet'* would go to the younger son. Marie-France was then able to cut her expenditure by dispensing with the services of both domestic help and chauffeur/gardener. An advertisement placed in the newsagents enabled her to soon find a local enthusiast keen to use the garden as a small holding and take timber from pruning the large trees for his wood burning stove. This was agreed at no charge in exchange for him maintaining the lawns and grounds.

Back in Paris, Rene Finot set up a standing order for payment of the monthly annuity, took out insurance against Marie-France living to a ripe old age and was content to sit back and wait. He had nothing against Marie-France who in fact reminded him of his late mother who had died the previous year at the age of 80. At 79, Marie-France was within a year of this sad event and Rene Finot had firm expectations of taking possession of 4, *rue Pied du Renard* in the none to distant future. He immersed himself in his work and his only contact with Marie-France was to ask his wife to remember to send her a card upon her 80th birthday.

Marie-France, despite her advancing age still enjoyed a bit of excitement. Although she had become disillusioned with horse racing she could usually be found at least two afternoons a week at the casino gaming tables. Roulette was her favourite. She had her 'lucky numbers' and tried and tested systems. To ensure she did not exceed her income, she was given a strict weekly allowance and her bank manager had a firm arrangement with the casino to refuse her credit. When she did occasionally land a big win her generosity always got the better of her and she insisted on buying everyone at or near the table a glass of champagne completely ignoring the fact that she had earlier lost most of her stake money. She rarely returned home with any winnings and continued to live only just within her means.

As the years went by Marie-France grew increasingly frail. Her mind slowly deteriorated and her memory lapses caused her to become forgetful. She lost the urge to leave her home and was content to be waited on hand and foot by her son and daughter-in-law. Initially they had found living with and looking after Marie-France a rewarding task. She was little trouble to them. Also, their house letting business proved to be a great success. They wished that they had embraced the tourism business much earlier in their lives. It was easier and less stressful than managing an established business and whilst income was not comparable they had neither responsibilities for other employees nor the thankless task of completing administrative paperwork. But they were ageing too and finding the demands of caring for Marie-France progressively demanding. They applied to Social Services and obtained the service of a nurse to attend twice a day to wash, feed and make Marie-France comfortable. As she passed 90 years of age, she was confined to a wheelchair during the day. It was placed next to her bed and she sat there comfortably, listening to the radio, watching television or more often than not, sleeping.

Rene Finot was gradually becoming impatient. For many years he had been able to afford to be sanguine about the matter but as Marie-France passed 92, Rene calculated that his total outgoings to date equalled the sum of the *'maison de maitre'* valuation thirteen years previously. The longer she lived the more he would be out of pocket. Now 59, he was one of the few people he knew of his age who was still working. Having made their money, most others had retired, some long ago, to live out the rest of their lives away from the bustle of Paris in a comfortable out of town house or apartment. So far he had been thwarted in his ambition to do the same. For the first time in his life he had had to admit defeat. The tenacious old lady had defied the statistical norms. He was aware of the expression - lies, damned lies and statistics - that he now found in this instance to be so true. Even worse was the ribbing he continually took from his remaining friends and acquaintances to whom he had often boasted of his future retirement as Lord of the Manor in the balmy climate of the South of France. They joked unmercifully at his expense. At restaurants, if the pheasant was a little overcooked they would say that it was a tough old bird but not as tough as his 'friend' Marie-France. If the fish was not to their taste, there was the inevitable reference to 'that stubborn old trout'.

When one of Rene's friends died suddenly following a skiing accident it focussed his attention upon his own health. If he died before Marie-France, his wife would have to continue with the annuity payments and if she failed to pay, the *'maison de maitre'* would be returned to Marie-France's ownership. Again, his friends capitalised on this. When wine glasses were being filled Rene only received a small amount as they laughingly reminded him that he must look after himself. When Rene once asked a friend how his grand-daughter had enjoyed the new sports car he had bought for her birthday, he received the reply that she had taken him out in it and it was the first time he had been taken for a ride by a woman! It was getting too much to bear.

By the time Marie-France was 95 she had already outlived the statistical probability of her death by twelve years. In addition to the *'bouquet'* the monthly annuity and land tax, Rene Finot had spent several thousand euros on building maintenance. With the benefit of hindsight he wished he had paid the asking price for the house at the time. What a fool he had been to allow his penchant for landing a bargain to get the better of him. For the first time in sixteen years he went to see her. Her son showed him into her room. She was asleep in her chair next to a radio with the sound turned to full pitch. The radio was switched off and the son tried to wake her. When she eventually opened her eyes she was bemused asking whom the gentleman was and why he had come to see her. Rene Finot tried to make polite conversation but to no avail. Marie-France evidently did not remember him. He noted that she looked pale and thin but came away with the realisation that suffering no stress and waited on hand and foot, she might continue to live for considerably longer.

The years rolled by without any obvious change in Marie-France's circumstances. She never left her room and just sat, ate, slept and was washed, cleaned and made comfortable. As her 100th birthday approached the family considered the possibility of a celebratory party but were reluctant to plan ahead in case Marie-France did not survive to see the day.

It was at this juncture that Rene Finot, browsing through news of the day, came across an article of a study carried out in Switzerland entitled '*Are you more likely to die on your birthday?*' It informed him that an analysis of deaths over a forty-year time span had concluded that people were 14% more likely to die on their birthday. There was something to suggest that people close to death 'hung on' until their birthday to achieve that milestone. Rene Finot saw this as the last chance to aspire to his coveted 'Lord of the Manor' status before he was too old himself to enjoy it.

He was the one person who had not been looking forward to Marie-France's hundredth birthday but having acknowledged long ago the loss of the statistical battle with her he had little else to lose. Two weeks before the likely event, he contacted the family and persuaded them to allow him to organise a garden party in honour of Marie-France. 100th birthdays were not now uncommon but it was nevertheless an achievement worthy of more than passing interest. Rene Finot would underwrite all the expenses if the family made the arrangements as per his instructions. He wanted as many of the family as possible to be present, the Mayor, civic dignitaries and other villagers to be invited and the press to be there in force. A marquee would be erected in the grounds and the best catering firm (*traiteur)* in the village contracted to put on a lavish spread. Most of all, the village's brass band, choir and accordionists would be engaged to facilitate dancing and general revelry. Rene Finot and his family intended to be in attendance when he would provide champagne, all the wines and other drinks for guests and also compare proceedings.

The family were more than pleased to accept this generous offer and enthusiastically set about putting Rene Finot's plans to good effect. As the great day approached they monitored Marie-France carefully explaining to her the significance of the event. She merely smiled and nodded her head giving the impression of a state of bliss whilst not being fully aware of exactly what was being prepared on her behalf. At least they were confident that she knew she was approaching 100 and would be alive and well on the day.

The 2nd of August 2010 proved to be one of the hottest days of the year. The temperature was forecast to exceed 34° centigrade and the scene was set for a long hot day of enjoyment, excitement and anticipation. Rene Finot and his wife, who were staying at a hotel in Nice, arrived early to direct events. A lunch had been arranged for over 150 guests in the marquee during which Marie-France would be brought down to hear the congratulatory speech of the Mayor and for the press to take photographs of her with family members.

Shortly before the meal, Rene Finot had been taken to see Marie-France but she was asleep in her wheelchair. He saw how frail she now was and wondered whether she knew it was her birthday. He was reassured when her family explained that they had spoken to her about it several times. Her youngest great-great granddaughter had been busy making a cake for the centenary event and he was finally convinced that she was fully aware of the occasion.

A nurse arrived at noon to wash and feed Marie-France following which she was wheeled down to the garden and into the marquee. Led by Rene Finot, guests stood in applause and the Mayor rose to make his speech. He gave a brief history of the village from the time Marie-France had been born - its prosperity then and its subsequent decline. Having recently been elected he vowed to restore the affluence Lodeza had once enjoyed.

Champagne was poured as a toast to Marie-France. The brass band struck up as the family gathered for photographs and the press surged forward to garner details of Marie-France's life. For over an hour, Marie-France remained in the marquee, quite awake and taking in every detail of the party atmosphere. As the nurse guided her back to her room, Rene Finot arranged for the band to play continuously under her window as loudly as possible. He wanted to be certain that she knew she had achieved centenarian status and maximise her realisation of the fact. The nurse left and Rene went up to see Marie-France. Before she fell asleep, he spoke loudly to her above the almost deafening sound of the brass band about the excitement of the day and persuaded her to take a glass of champagne with him. To his satisfaction she gulped the first glass down and surprised him by gesturing for another that she soon greedily consumed. She hadn't taken alcohol for ten years but her taste for good champagne remained. She then settled back in her chair and fell into a deep asleep. When the night nurse returned in the early evening she could not waken Marie-France. There was evidence of breathing but it was somewhat irregular and shallow. Everyone was concerned at their inability to rouse her and wondered if the birthday excitement had been too much for her to take. Rene Finot had remained in the background but upon hearing the news suggested that a priest be called. Had his devious ploy worked, had Marie-France just been waiting to achieve her 100th birthday, would he become 'Lord of the Manor' at long last?

Failing to arouse her, the priest also expressed anxiety at Marie-France's condition and immediately called the doctor. It was soon diagnosed that Marie-France's heart was strong and that she was suffering from the deadening effects of an excess of alcohol. When that wore off she would, in the doctor's opinion, fully recover and continue to live for several more years. Once again, the startling statistic that death was much more likely on a birthday than any other day of the year had been disproved in this instance by Marie-France. She was truly a remarkable old lady.

Rene and Justine Finot returned to their hotel in Nice and spent the next fortnight viewing properties on the Cote d'Azure, eventually settling for a large apartment within a complex managed by a *'concierge'* containing a communal pool and tennis courts. The ample grounds were well maintained and the specimen trees, shrubs and flowers provided a pleasant countryside oasis within a few metres of a busy promenade. Even though the property was owned by an elderly widow who was moving to a nursing home Rene Finot did not mention the possibility of a *Viager*. His wife was delighted with the property and he was content to pay the asking price. His fingers had been burnt once and he did not intend a repeat.

The couple alternated between their Paris home and Nice apartment, enjoying the autumn and winter weather in the South. It was over five years later that Rene Finot received the telephone call he had been awaiting for 26 long years. Marie-France Delfort had passed away in her sleep in her 106th year. He was now the official owner of 4, *rue Pied du Renard*, Lodiza.

As he contacted his bank to cancel the *Viager* annuity standing order he knew that he had paid out more than twice the original value of the property. But his 'Lord of the Manor' dream had ended long before and the family would never take up residence there.

Once Marie-France's eldest son and daughter-in-law had moved back to their house, Rene contacted an estate agent to arrange the sale. He did have some consolation when he received a lump sum from the insurance company on the policy he had taken out against Marie-France living beyond predicted age. At least that had been a sound investment.

But there was to be a pleasant surprise in store for him. Under the new Mayor's drive and implementation of initiatives, Lodiza had gradually been developing into a prime residential as well as tourist attraction. Now, there were excellent communications with nearby Nice and Cannes. Many people had recently decided to settle in the area to enjoy life in the beautiful countryside a mere stones throw from the busy beaches, traffic jams and parking problems all along the coast. The village had become a magnet for people seeking retirement homes and, with a shortage of prime properties, prices were at a premium. When the estate agent telephoned to say he had received an offer in excess of valuation, Rene Finot knew he was about to make a substantial profit. He called out joyfully to his wife, "In honour of Marie-France and the Mayor of Lodiza, we should celebrate by booking a table at the Cagnes-sur-Mer racecourse restaurant for this evenings meeting."

THE PORTRAIT

It would be difficult to imagine two people as diverse as Charles Colbert and Jacques Grandcloud. Now well past eighty, they had, against the odds been firm friends since their teenage years.

Charles, born of a well-to-do family with old Parisian connections had been given every opportunity for advancement - extra tuition, the best equipment and attire for what was hoped would be a successful sporting and business career. But life at home had been too easy with the services of a nanny and domestic help. By his early teens he had developed into a tall, stocky, smartly attired youth but indolent and lazy to a fault. Far from attaining the desired heights, he had eschewed all forms of physical exercise, considering himself a young man of leisure, an only son and heir to the not inconsiderable family fortune. Fond of company and a good conversationalist, life as a gentleman of independent means beckoned.

Sent to a private school, Charles with a good brain, showed little inclination to use it. On one occasion, the Headmaster wrote a personal letter to Charles' parents requesting them to visit his office to discuss the boys' future. As the letter forcibly pointed out 'that with his present attitude, your son is wasting not only his own time but also the valuable time of the school's staff '.

Jacques on the other hand came from a deprived background. Looked after by his widowed mother, there was little money to spare once the rent of their small two-bedroom flat had been paid. Food, heat and lighting were by necessity in short supply and with two elder sisters making constant demands, Jacques often had to fend for himself, soon realising that effort and hard work were the key to rising above the poverty level into which he had been born. Small and wiry he was nevertheless gregarious with boundless energy constantly on the lookout for advancement and social opportunities.

Throughout his secondary school years, Jacques remained anchored in the bottom form, struggling to grasp even basic principles of core subjects. Like Charles, he was soon written off by his tutors and year-end reports made dismal reading. The only recorded event of note on Jacques report was a quote from the headmaster that 'I am informed by the art master that Jacques spends most of his lessons doodling, his saving grace being a natural artistic skill that in years ahead might just stand him in good stead'.

As opposite poles attract, it was this gulf in background and character that was the catalyst for their friendship. Finding themselves unemployed at sixteen in the Atlantic coastal town of *Oeunes-sur-Mer* they were drawn together by their love of conversation and a passionate interest in motor bikes and cars.

Having left school without qualifications, they met when both joined the resort's go-kart club to indulge their love of speed, competition, and excitement. In their very first competitive race, they formed a fierce rivalry, each giving everything in an effort to attain superiority. Charles, with money to burn could afford to race each and every day whereas Jacques had spent weeks gathering sufficient funds for just one race. Despite Jacques' will to succeed, Charles' experience won the day, but he had to acknowledge just what a determined character Jacques Grandcloud was.

Their friendship blossomed, Charles loaning Jacques his spare motor bike for outings together when they spoke of their desire to obtain a full driving licence as soon as possible.

During this time, Charles did no work, daily practising the skills of driving with an old family car in a field adjacent to his home. Jacques was encouraged by his former art master to attend his evening classes but still had plenty of time to walk to Charles' home to sample driving experience himself.

From his early days, Charles was well read and could hold his own in reasoned debate. Jacques was a poor reader with a low level of knowledge and aggressively self-opinionated. Rarely a day passed when they did not meet to discuss, tussle and argue over world affairs. Jacques was dogged in his insistence of being absolutely right and it was usually Charles who eventually gave way to whom he mockingly called 'his little expert'.

They argued constantly, Charles in his measured, cultivated tone often drowned out by Jacques deep, loud, combative voice. Any casual observer could have been excused for thinking that they were sworn enemies such was the intensity of their arguments. They often tried to reason with one another but their demeanour quickly became ruffled, descending into contradictory statements and violent, threatening gestures. They shouted at the tops of their voices and challenged each others views to such a degree that they had to be pulled apart as they wrestled on the ground. Yet for all that, their poise soon returned and they laughed with one another clasping hands in friendship, parting to return home in good spirits.

For the next fifteen years their careers blossomed, Charles with family connections obtained a number of taxi licences and Jacques became a long distance lorry driver, supplementing his income by occasionally providing humorous sketches for local papers, magazines and pamphlets on a freelance basis.

Charles, being the character he was, worked as little as possible, shunning low-fare local journeys, concentrating upon longer, lucrative hospital or airport runs. His business acumen and ready family support saw him consolidate this enterprise. He was able to pick and choose those special clients whom he wished to escort personally.

Jacques' long distance driving took him all over Europe. His thrifty nature enabled him to save sufficiently in anticipation of a future less onerous occupation.

Whenever the occasion arose they met to socialise, eat and drink in the local bistros and restaurants. They were best man at each other's weddings and godparents to their subsequent children. The respective wives were always there to sooth things over when high-spirited arguments appeared to be getting out of hand but as always, evenings ended with genuine handshakes and friendly backslapping.

By their mid thirties, the two friends were able to realise their true ambitions. Charles sold his taxi licences for a very substantial profit and went to work as chauffeur for the chairman of a large aircraft company. His was a prestigious post with full official uniform and a serviced fleet of Rolls Royces at his ready disposal. The job took him to the many capital cities of Europe. These he relished most of all, especially trips to Germany where he was able to indulge his passion for high speed driving on sections of unrestricted autobahns. Occasional overseas travel was always by first-class flights. On one trip to Cuba, Charles took a liking to hand-rolled Havana cigars. They became his trademark and when at leisure in drinking establishments would invariably be seen smoking one. For twenty-five years he worked for four different chairmen and became a confident to all. They spoke to and treated him as an equal. The job had drawbacks, his being on-call until meetings, often lasting until well into the early hours, were concluded, and necessarily abstaining from alcohol during this time. There were however benefits that more than compensated for these great deprivations. Being privy to much business gossip and rumour he took advantage of information received to speculate on the stock market and by the time of his retirement had accumulated an impressive share portfolio and considerable wealth.

Jacques' change took him in the opposite direction. Gone were the long days of road travel. Retiring from his driving job, he rented an artists studio in the centre of *Oeunes-sur-Mer*, something to which he had always aspired. Having an eye for detail and a keen knowledge of form and shape, his unfailing sense of humour fitted him to be a caricaturist. From early school-days, even the most exasperated teachers had admired his doodles in class. They had concluded that if all else failed he would always be able to earn a living through this medium and with the later encouragement of his art master; his true destiny was about to be realised. He had natural talent, no more obvious than his ability to effortlessly draw a perfect circle on the ground at the start of a game of *pétanque*. For thirty years he dedicated himself to his task, accumulating a large and diverse stock of artworks. He painted serious portraits in oil; landscapes, seascapes, feature buildings in watercolour and caricatures in various ranges of graphite pencil. For his own pleasure, he produced detailed portraits of all the Presidents of the Fifth *République*. Being staunchly left wing, his favourites were the two socialist Presidents of that era. To make up for what he considered to be a shameful lack of representation, he also sketched a large number of portraits of several socialist Mayors of local communities together with various national union and social leaders whom he idolised. His landscapes were varied, depicting the local countryside - castles of *Aquitaine*, *Dordogne* village rooftops, forested areas in *Landes* or glorious coastal seascapes.

His main source of income that barely covered his expenditure was from individual caricatures of local people - friends, acquaintances and others who wished to be portrayed in the pleasing manner that bore the distinct trademark of Jacques Grandcloud's individuality.

An unconventional dresser who always whatever the weather, sported a black leather wide brimmed hat and matching black leather jacket with an open necked white shirt, his persona totally represented his style. With boundless energy and a jaunty walk he could often be seen in the early morning with a hand rolled cigarette between his lips making his way to a nearby jetty to fish for mackerel using cherry tomatoes as bait. A couple of hours were usually sufficient for him to land a good catch. This and produce from his garden, helped eke out the family budget.

Gradually, Jacques' paintings and sketches were more than sufficient for him to be able to mount exhibitions at various small art galleries around town. He was in the habit of photocopying a sample of his works, placing them in an album small enough to be carried in his inside jacket pocket. When out drinking with Charles, he had an disarming way of producing the album and successfully convincing potential clients that for a small commission they too could become part of his growing collection. So great became his output that over the years, town halls, restaurants, cafés and sporting clubs over a wide area displayed one or more of his caricatures. The imitation of the individual with the large head and truncated body exaggerated his or her characteristics with comic effect. Drawn in such stunning detail with close observation of features and subtle shading, the full personality of the sitter was instantly apparent.

Charles joined in the general banter that arose when Jacques was trying to gently persuade a possible customer to agree to a commission.

"Don't listen to him," he would taunt. "Jacques' work is clever but not worth the price he demands."

They would argue fiercely about the merits of the work.

"What do you know about fine art?" Jacques would retort. "Nothing at all. You keep to your flash cars, big cigars, stocks and shares and leave creative matters to me."

Jacques usually won the day and commissions continued to roll in. After the umpteenth argument on the same theme, Charles would chide Jacques.

"All right my little expert, if your caricatures are so good and so sought after, do one of me; after all I am your best friend."

Jacques set to work at once and in due course produced a caricature of Charles depicting him with uncanny accuracy. A smiling Charles in open-necked floral shirt, holding a cigarette in one hand, with the other pointing towards his winning *'boule'* nearest the little *'cochonnet'*.

"A bargain at €100 and I'll throw in the frame," said Jacques, presenting the caricature to him.

"€100?" queried Charles. "Why would I want to pay €100 for that? It doesn't even show me with my favourite cigar," continued an unimpressed Charles.

"You asked me to draw you. I think it's a very good likeness and one of my best works. €100 is my standard fee," replied Jacques.

"I didn't say I would pay you," retorted Charles. "I said I was your best friend and best friends should look after one another not resort to extortion."

"You wealthy Conservatives are all the same," shouted Jacques back at him. "You expect other people to work for nothing whilst you just play around living a life of luxury and leisure."

"The trouble with you, my little expert, is that you always criticise people who have done well in life and never give credit for their achievements. You only want to bring them down to your impoverished level instead of aspiring to match their success. You can keep you caricature. What would I want with it? When I die, my relatives would only throw it out of the house with the rest of my belongings," was Charles' sharp rejoinder.

A furious Jacques recovered his work of art. He had received a request to put on an exhibition of his works in the town's community hall and Charles' caricature would be just another one to be added to those he had earmarked for display.

The community hall was a vast rectangular room, so spacious that it took over 200 of Jacques' various works to give it an art gallery feel. In addition to many of his caricatures, several of which he had temporarily borrowed back from their owners for the occasion, he included a selection of his oil portraits and watercolours. For those works not already sold, he produced a brochure with a short description of the subject and sale price.

The official opening of the exhibition commenced with an introductory speech by the Mayor followed by general viewing of the exhibits, concluding with complimentary participation in a buffet and sampling of regional wines provided by a local *viticulteur*. Such occasions were generally regarded as for social and promotional purposes. The many onlookers enjoyed viewing exhibits but few were art lovers. Food was eaten down to the last crumb; wine drunk down to the last drop and everyone went home happy and contented if somewhat unsteady on their feet. But it was rare for anyone to buy a work of art.

On this occasion however, the Mayor was conscious of the need for an appropriate gift from the town to the President of the *République* to mark the occasion of an official visit arranged for the following month.

Jacques' portrait of the current President had taken him six painstaking weeks to finish to his complete satisfaction. It was so fresh and lifelike that upon seeing an asking price of just €250, the Mayor had no qualms about spending public funds upon what he considered both a bargain and a fitting tribute to the town's honoured guest. It was the highest priced sale Jacques had ever made!

At the conclusion of the visit when the Mayor proudly presented the painting by one of his own townsfolk to the President of the *République*, press photographers clamoured to take pictures of the President accepting his portrait. The likeness was uncanny.

Photographs appeared in national and local newspapers and in several society magazines. Many in the art world were given to asking of the artist's name and soon Jacques became something of a celebrity, in constant demand to accept commissions for portraits from society people of wealth and influence. Despite being pitched into the limelight and experiencing extreme pressures occasioned by instant fame, he continued with his work with the same painstaking detail, still charging his original rates. The only concessions he made were to terminate his fishing and gardening activities.

When it became known that Jacques' painting of the President was displayed in a prominent position within the *Elysée Palace*, art dealers and connoisseurs vied for his attention.

The Mayor was also a well-known local benefactor and contacted Jacques with a proposal to raise money for a local charity. A man with influential contacts and friends, the Mayor's idea was to request a number of both established and up and coming artists to exhibit in his private gallery before an invited audience, a dozen or so of their works at normal selling price. If sold, the artist was guaranteed 75% of the purchase price with 25% donated to the charity. Jacques agreed on condition that having little business acumen, the Mayor would choose those of his works thought eminently saleable and price them accordingly. Ten of Jacques works were selected, including his caricature of Charles. When Jacques read the brochure that had been prepared and forwarded to invited guests, he was astounded by the guide prices. His oils were priced between €5,000 to €12,000, land and seascapes from €2,000 to €8,000 and the Charles caricature at €1,000.

As a resident of known financial standing, Charles was one of the *invités* amongst a large gathering of art lovers, business people, charitable supporters and moneyed people who just liked to be seen to mingle and participate in the affairs of such exalted company.

Past experience had told the Mayor that as soon as one guest was known to have bought a painting, intense rivalry and one-upmanship guaranteed that the rest would strive to outdo one another. As the evening progressed, five of Jacques works, although in his opinion astronomically valued by his own standards, were soon to find eager buyers. Many guests made complimentary remarks upon the uncanny likeness of Jacques portrait of Charles, but Charles himself was unmoved. He had once rejected the work for €100 so why would he want to pay ten times as much? He was however a person who had learned from and profited by not making the same mistake twice. A realisation that Jacques' work was in demand and could eventually be internationally recognised within the upper echelon of artistic merit persuaded him that an investment opportunity was beckoning. People were clamouring for Jacques' works and before the evening was over, Charles had made out his cheque to the Mayors Fund citing his action to be 'in the interest of worthwhile charitable causes'.

The event raises over €40,000 for charity and Jacques received a personal cheque for €18,000!

Charles hung his caricature in the hallway of his home and made sure that it was adequately insured. Who knew what value it might eventually attain? It seemed that anyone who was anyone wished to own a 'Jacques Grandcloud' and would pay whatever it took to acquire one. Charles, knowing of Jacques naivety of the operation of supply and demand offered to help price his works. He had an interest and wished to see his investment grow. Jacques, too busy to argue the point, accepted his offer. Over the years Charles looked on in satisfaction at the steady price rise Jacques' works commanded and the money rolled in.

"I suppose by now you must be a millionaire," surmised Charles, "and as I have helped make you one I think I'm entitled to some commission. What do you say my little expert?"

"Commission?" queried Jacques. " Why would I want to pay my best friend commission? You know that best friends do things from the goodness of their heart because they are best friends. Didn't you once tell me that? And if I am a millionaire, it's only down to people like you with too much money to spend. You once said my works were not worth the price I was asking. You were wrong then but now if you made the same observation, I would fully agree with you. Nothing has changed in the way I draw and paint; the rent of my studio is the same as ever and my materials are inexpensive."

"Ah, on the contrary despite what you say, much has changed," replied Charles. "I have mockingly called you 'my little expert' because every time we have had a discussion, you have repeatedly maintained your position and despite overwhelming odds against, have never had the sense to concede. To avoid conflict, I have always given way thinking that one day you will see the light. But even at this late stage in our lives, your obstinate streak remains. Let me tell you why you have been so successful in the last few years. Despite your cantankerous nature, people - and I include myself here - have come to recognise your talent, your gift of being able to produce work that they recognise as requiring special skills. Not only do they like what they see, they consider your art form to be something that will have lasting value. It takes a special type of person to recognise talent. People with foresight and money - and again I include myself - are continuously on the lookout for sound investments, things that will not only preserve their wealth but enable it to grow. I can see you doubting me but just consider investments in such as contemporary works of art, vintage wines, postage stamps, rare first editions even letters by famous people. The material price is negligible but the resale value is often many millions. Perhaps you are not yet in that exalted category but take it from me your works are in great demand my little expert. The caricature I purchased at that charity exhibition has since increased in value many times over and I have bought several more of your works since."

Jacques for once made no reply. Later that week, he made an appointment with his bank manager whom he had trusted to handle his financial affairs. Even after paying all taxes due and management fees, he was astounded by the amount that had accumulated in his various accounts. Recognising the contribution Charles had made to his life he had no hesitation in making out a substantial cheque for his best friend.

Fame and fortune did not change Jacques' outlook in any way. Still of the jaunty stride, unconventional dress and optimistic outlook, he left all financial matters to his advisor's. Going about the business of enjoying life to the full, he was happy to work hard in his creative way, to meet people, talk, argue, eat, drink and smoke.
Despite their many differences, Charles and Jacques' strong bond of friendship survived numerous stresses and strains and continued throughout their lives.
Following the death of his wife, Charles remarked that the one thing that kept him going was not the fact that he was a rich, successful man but the pleasure of Jacques' company.

When Charles suddenly succumbed to a heart attack at the age of eighty-two, his family immediately went to clear all furnishings and belongings as a prelude to selling the house.
His caricature, still hanging in pride of place in the hallway was removed and unceremoniously thrown into a box of items bound for a charity shop. Commented his son, "I never liked that awful cartoon of Dad. I don't know whatever possessed him to buy it!"

REMEMBERING MASLOW

Janine Duval had studied Maslow's theory of motivation pyramid in her early years as part of a psychology course. It was one of those pieces of information touched on at school or university such as refraction, stress/strain equations or the law of diminishing returns that unless you followed a particular profession, you never found a use for again throughout your entire life.

Being a keen gardener, photosynthesis had been a useful source of knowledge but Maslow was but a distant memory. Janine vaguely recalled that the theory started with basic physiological needs progressing upwards to encompass status, recognition, action and wisdom.

Although she had obviously never encountered anyone with the rare intellect of a Leonardo da Vinci, Shakespeare, Beethoven or Einstein it hadn't struck her that elements of the theory had already touched her life. Her late husband had been privileged to be awarded the National Order of Merit near the end of his career when President of the Institute of Quarrying. They had both put that down to his being in the right place at the right time and had regarded it as recognition of the Institute rather than himself. Nevertheless, it had done his prestige no harm at all and on the strength of it he had gone on to write an acclaimed book on the subject of limestone quarrying.

It wasn't until some years later that Janine came to realise both the importance of being in the right place at the right time and the full significance of Maslow's theory.

For ten years a widow, Janine lived alone in a large detached house on a narrow road near the centre of Claremontville, a medium sized town and important administrative centre in South-West France. Always a Conservative by nature Janine had been proud of the fact that on the political map, her town had stood out as a small oasis of blue surrounded entirely by a sea of red. 'A bastion of free enterprise and culture' she liked to think, 'and long may it continue.'

It hadn't continued and she had been appalled when at the last election, a young Socialist upstart had defeated the incumbent mayor of thirty years standing. It wasn't quite the end of the world but for Janine it promised to be a harbinger of increased taxes, more unwarranted strikes as unions exercised their power, followed by social unrest.

But life had to go on and Janine was appreciative of the quality of her life in her smart, upper class road where all the properties were of differing designs, large, well maintained, expensive and highly desirable. The exterior of her house was painted white and abutted the pavement next to the road that was just wide enough for two cars to pass.

Janine's reaquaintance with Maslow's theory started with what appeared to be a trivial incident. Returning from town one Tuesday afternoon, she was displeased to see a large open-back lorry parked within inches of her pristine white front wall. Motorists occasionally parked on the pavement but only for a short time whilst they visited other residents and then they were gone. Next morning, she was surprised and annoyed to find the lorry still there. Worst of all, on the open back was a large oil tank with a screw cap hanging loose from the top. The stench of diesel oil was almost unbearable and as Janine inspected the vehicle, it made her stomach turn. She quickly observed that although the insurance notice was current, the tax disc was three months out of date, the tyres bald, the front headlights broken, the wipers damaged and the windscreen full of cracks and indentations. Although the driver's side door was locked the passenger door was not. There was no ignition key.

She hoped against hope that someone would arrive to drive away the offending vehicle. No one knew anything about it. It just seemed to have arrived. Some neighbours even thought that Janine owned it and asked if she would move it as its unsightly appearance lowered the tone of the neighbourhood!

By Friday morning, she decided she must report the matter to the police. Just before lunch she went to the office of *La Gendarmerie Nationale* in the town centre. There, a middle-aged lady clerical officer attended to her. She busily took down details of Janine's name and address, make and registration number of the problem vehicle and promised to instruct an officer to deal with the matter.

When nothing had happened by the following Wednesday, Janine made a return visit to *La Gendarmerie Nationale* office. This time a uniformed *Lieutenant de Police* saw her.

When she said she had reported her complaint the previous Friday morning he replied very seriously, "Ah *Madame,* that was a bad time to come. Over the long weekend, we have been supervising security for our Spanish Festival and I'm afraid that an abandoned vehicle would not be a priority."

He rummaged through a bundle of papers on his desk.

"Whom did you say you saw?" he demanded.

"A middle-aged dark haired lady who was sitting there," responded Janine pointing at a chair next to a leather-topped desk on the far side of the room.

"Must have been one of our part-time civilian officers," he mumbled.

"Can't find any report among these papers so we'd better start again." Janine repeated the information. The *Lieutenant* wrote it down longhand and promised to send someone to assess the problem.

"Rest assured *Madame*, once we have been informed of a difficulty such as this we are obliged to follow it up," he said confidently.

On Friday morning, a uniformed officer arrived at her house and surveyed the lorry. "How long has it been here?" he questioned.

"Ten days now," responded Janine. "Surely it must be abandoned? Look at the state of it, the lack of taxation, not to mention the foul smell of diesel oil."

The policeman had another look and then concluded, "Not much we can do *Madame*. As the lorry was driven here it is obviously roadworthy and it is still possible that the owner will return to drive it away. Maybe it is just broken down. We could contact the vehicle removal firm to tow it to the abandoned vehicle pound but that will take at least fifteen days. Best thing is to leave it for a while and see what develops."

Nothing developed. The weekend came and went. The smell of diesel oil from the lorry intensified in the hot summer sunshine to the extent that it permeated the whole of the immediate area. It prevented Janine from enjoying the pleasure of her garden. Confined inside with the windows firmly closed, she received regular telephone calls from disgruntled neighbours asking what if any progress she had made with the authorities.

Then, she thought of a possible solution. If the powers that be were incapable of action then she would take matters into her own hands. The lorry next to her wall was parked on a slight incline. Later that evening, under the cover of darkness but assisted by the glow of a nearby streetlamp, she went outside. Squeezing through the narrow gap between her house wall and the lorry, she opened the passenger door and climbed into the cab. She wriggled across to the drivers seat and loosened the handbrake. Slowly, the lorry began to roll backwards. It was Janine's plan that she could turn the steering wheel anti-clockwise and guide the lorry into the centre of the road when she would re-apply the handbrake and leave it stranded there. From the glow of the streetlamp, any approaching vehicle would easily see it but would not be able to pass. Then the authorities would have to be called to do something urgently. However, the steering column was locked and she could not turn the wheel. All she achieved was to roll the vehicle back towards her front door and a lamp post that would have halted the lorry's progress, denying her access to her own house. Realising the futility of her exercise, she swiftly re-applied the handbrake and halted the lorry just before it covered her front door. Frustratingly, she had made her predicament worse and now she had only just sufficient room to access her property.

Her patience exhausted, next day on the advice of a neighbour, she angrily made her way this time to the *Police Municipale*. Explaining the situation, she demanded to see the Chief of Police and was eventually shown into an office with the nameplate *'Brigadier'* emblazoned on the door. At last she thought, someone of substance and influence. She remembered the pride she had felt when her son had obtained a post with a multi-international organisation in Chicago and had informed her that he held the title of Vice-President. Upon visiting his workplace, she soon discovered that this title seemed to apply to most employees almost as far down the hierarchy to the shirt-sleeved doorman. "With me, Mum," he had said, "it's the challenge that counts but with most of these guys, they need a title to make them feel important and hide their inadequacies."

Her initial euphoria was short-lived when she watched the *Brigadier* himself proceed to type a full report of the offending lorry incident using a very old typewriter.

"This will go straight into the system," he said confidently, passing a copy to her. "I've been in the police force for twenty years and can assure you that action will be taken, *Madame.*"

On her way out, Janine noticed that the two adjacent doors had brass plates attached bearing the titles *"Brigadier-Chef"* and *"Major de Police"* so maybe her man, like those at the Chicago multi-international, was none too important after all!

Nevertheless, a police vehicle pulled up outside her house the very next day and four policemen alighted to begin inspecting the lorry. One rang her doorbell and when she appeared, started to ask the same questions as the officer who had visited the previous Friday. They took notes, but making no observations or suggestions soon returned to their car and drove off.

The weekend arrived without further contact or action. Neighbours complained to her continually about the foul smell of diesel oil in a manner that implied it was her own fault. She tried to explain to them the steps she had taken and how she was relying upon the police to take necessary action,

"What else can I do?" she appealed to them. "I've been to both the *Gendarmerie Nationale* and *Police Municipale* without success."

"Hmm," muttered one neighbour.

"I have experience of the workings of the police force. They are civil servants, under-worked, overstaffed, overpaid and looking forward to early retirement on gold-plated pensions. Their day is invariably as follows: -

8.30	Arrive for work. Take files from cupboards.
9.0	Peruse papers taken from files.
10.0	Coffee break
11.0	Type a couple of reports, shuffle papers around, replace in files, lock away
12.0	Lunch
14.0	Take files from cupboards, place papers on desk.

14.30   Coffee break
15.0   Go to minor road with speed radar gun.
16.30   Back to office to write report
17.30   Return papers to files, lock away and go home.

This system meets their lifelong needs. They have guaranteed job security, live a safe contented life and have friendships within their own group of likeminded people. They are happy in their own little cocooned world. I have observed them with their speed radar gun. When a vehicle is considered to exceed the speed limit, they blow a whistle to attract the driver! It is like something out of the *Keystone Cops* ancient movies. All that technology and they rely upon a whistle! And as soon as they are gone, the traffic reverts to its normal routine of excessive speeds. Many officers are good people who initially want to do well but are held back by inertia within the service. They assume the role of social service officers rather than a dynamic force dedicated to upholding the law. I doubt if you will get any action from them because the system does not allow them to be motivated to do anything more.

The neighbour was right and the lorry remained in its unwanted position outside Janine's house. On Monday morning, twenty-one days after the lorry had first appeared Janine rang the *Police Nationale* complaining bitterly of the lack of attention to her reported problem. In the afternoon, two further uniformed officers appeared and proceeded to ask the same questions as their predecessors.

"You are the sixth and seventh officers to visit me," she complained, completely exasperated by this time.

"Do you not co-ordinate things in your office?" She showed them her copy of the report completed with the *Brigadier*. They sympathised and made to leave but not before telling her pointedly that they had a very long list of abandoned vehicles and it would take weeks for the abandoned vehicle brigade to get round to her small problem.

"First of all I'm told it will be fifteen days. It's already three weeks since the dirty old lorry was parked here and now you tell me it will be several more weeks before you get around to doing something. We pay a huge amount of habitation tax in this town and seem to get little service for our money," she despaired.

The situation remained unresolved by next Saturday morning when Janine was preparing to attend a civil baptism. She had been invited by two friends to come along to the Town Hall to witness the baptism of their young son that was to be performed by the Mayor at a civil ceremony. Arranged for 11 am, it was to be followed by lunch for all invited guests. Janine, in her best dress and hat decided to walk to the Town Hall and made sure she had placed plenty of perfume in her handbag in order to eliminate the possible smell of diesel oil on her clothes. It was another warm, sunny day and she arrived at the Town Hall about ten minutes before the event. The authorities had recently changed the venue for wedding and baptism ceremonies and all the other guests had proceeded to the former venue only to be re-routed to the new location. Consequently, Janine found herself alone with the Mayor and his secretary awaiting arrival of the main party. The Mayor came across, introduced himself to Janine and suggested they wait outside in the cooler air of the adjacent courtyard. Janine was surprised by his easy, friendly manner and warmed to him immediately. After a few seconds of small talk Janine plucked up courage to tell the Mayor that she had a *'petit problem'* that he might possibly be able to resolve. She recounted her woes following arrival of the abandoned lorry and her meetings with the police that had produced no positive results. "I'm at my wits end *Monsieur le Maire*. I've tried all possible avenues open to me without the slightest success. It's been almost a month. I've been to both *La Gendarmerie Nationale* and the *Police Municipale* several times, spoken to them by telephone, signed a typed report and had seven different policemen visit my house. Despite this, nothing has happened and I've been given no information whatsoever. I've no idea to whom the vehicle is registered and do not know what enquiries if any the police have made. My neighbours are also complaining about the awful smell and the fact that they are unable to park their cars opposite this lorry, as there is insufficient room on the road for vehicles to pass. Do you think you could possibly help? I don't know what else I can do."

The Mayor, who had recently been elected as the first Socialist to hold office in Claremontville asked her to write down her name and address on a piece of paper provided by his secretary. Then, he took his mobile phone from his pocket, pressed a number and began to talk. He walked out of the courtyard towards his private office and was not seen again until well after all the other guests had arrived. The start of the ceremony was delayed for several minutes until the smiling Mayor reappeared. He duly conducted the service; spoke of the interesting history of civil baptisms in France, finally placing a commemorative medal around the neck of the young boy.

Obviously running late and having a wedding ceremony to perform for a nervous young couple and a large number of waiting guests, the Mayor was unable to attend lunch at the boy's parent's home nearby.

During the celebrations, a considerable amount of food and drink was consumed before Janine departed for home satisfied and happy at the day's events.

She strolled slowly back home, enjoying the warmth of the late afternoon sunshine. As she rounded the corner of her road, she had to blink several times in surprise and delight before fully realising that the offending lorry had gone! It was a strange thing that no one had seen the lorry arrive and no one appeared to have seen it depart. Yet, it had been there for almost four weeks and had caused Janine a great deal of trouble and heartache. All of a sudden, it seemed like a distant memory. Her contentment with life knew no bounds as she surveyed her road, which miraculously had been returned to normal.

She was thankful that she had had the good fortune like her late husband all those years ago to be in the right place at the right time and to meet a man of stature and influence. None of the dreadful things she had envisaged following the election of a Socialist Mayor had happened and he had proved to be a very smartly dressed, charming fellow. Yes, he accorded truly to Maslow's needs pyramid and was accomplished at making things happen. It was he she had to thank for cutting through all the red tape and rousting up all those complacent administrative non-entities.

Previously a proud Conservative she had no hesitation in changing the habits of a lifetime. At the next Mayoral election she rejected the Conservative candidates paper and placed a firm cross on the paper of the Socialist Mayor in recognition of what she was sure had been his greatest achievement.

Story 13 - Democracy or Hypocricy?

THE TALE OF 'THE RAT'

1

Democracy was once described as allowing someone to pick your pocket and choosing the person to do it. A cynical view maybe but possibly with a grain of truth?

Let us take for example the extraordinary events surrounding successive municipal elections in the French town of Bonnetocque as personally experienced by Steven and Joyce Fenbridge.

Steven and Joyce had enjoyed many a summer at their holiday home in the town, so much so that they decided to sell their main house in England and move permanently to Bonnetocque.

You may ask the whereabouts of Bonnetocque and why anyone from England would wish to move there permanently? Suffice to say, it is a small town of fifty odd thousand population set in the middle of rolling countryside - fields with row upon row of boring, dull coloured vines, interspersed in summer by glorious splashes of wild red poppies and commercially grown yellow sunflower or rape-seed crops. It's main attractions - well known to Steven and Joyce - were warm summer sunshine, spacious affordable housing and a relaxed lifestyle aided by an abundance of surprisingly decent wine. It's drawbacks, costly rates and - as yet unknown to them - corrupt politicians. Corruption and politics are two words which some think go inexorably together and as the story progresses, you may be convinced, if you are not already so, that this is the norm nowadays.

One of the first things Steven and Joyce did in Bonnetocque was to take their required documents to the Town Hall to register as voters. They provided their passports for proof of identity and nationality, a utility bill to verify their address, French tax returns, health cards and attestations in case all else failed and, after much scrutiny, finally allowed to complete a voter registration form. They were now registered as eligible to vote in local mayoral and European elections if not for the President.

Invariably, as British citizens are oft to boast, Steven and Joyce Fenbridge quoted British democracy as the best in the world and an example to all. They recalled the struggles to obtain basic representation; the Ballot Act's of yesteryear and the fight of woman suffragettes for recognition. Now, everyone had the right to vote for his or her chosen representative and both were adamant that they should use it. It was impossible for them to envisage any other system guaranteed to provide for expression of people's wishes in such a fair and just manner.

True, they had heard of and read about various underhand practices in some parts of the world. Rigging of voting systems, stuffing ballot boxes with fraudulent votes and bribery of influential people were some of the ploys regularly reported. Then followed the inevitable practice of losers challenging the results, citing corruption on a large scale. Independent election monitors usually found irrefutable evidence of such wilful dishonesty, but rarely was anything done. But these were confined to megalomaniac dictators or oppressive regimes in far off lands and were not the concern of long established European nations who conformed to the Rule of Law. Or were they?

Steven and Joyce had to wait three years before their first French municipal election. As a young man, Steven had experienced the success of the British system having taken part in election duties as poll clerk and later as deputy returning officer in charge of the vote and count at a principal ward. He understood all the legal niceties of operating an election in a fair and transparent manner from initial voter verification to final acceptance of the result by all candidates. Steven and Joyce placed great reliance upon this system. They believed that democracy was additionally guaranteed by the pride and honesty of the representative's themselves. In his formative years, Steven had listened to a colourful political speech by a well known, no nonsense Member of Parliament who had described the security surrounding the voting system as 'copper bottomed guaranteed, and as watertight as a duck's arse'.

They soon discovered the French way of doing things. Promotional leaflets inundated their letterbox from seven competing parties for election to the council, including that of our 'hero', the current Mayor, *M. Maximillion Ratti* (hereinafter known as 'THE RAT'). They represented all shades of the political spectrum from far-right National Front to ultra-left Trotskyites (yes, there are still some alive and kicking in France).

As determined for a town of its size, Bonnetocque had 47 council members and each party listed their leader (the potential Mayor) and 46 other representatives in order of preference. To ensure equality, the names were alternatively male-female or female-male. Joyce thought that to be very fair and so enlightened for France, a country that until 1945 had been one of the last to recognise that women possessed the intelligence to vote!

They each received their official voting cards through the post, with seven foolscap-sized papers in different colours representing each party.

On the first ballot, registered electors were to vote for one of the seven parties. If one received more than 50% of the vote, it would be elected. At this stage, I will not bore you with the mathematics of the allocation system other than to say that, without giving the victor all the seats, it would be very difficult to envisage anything so highly geared in favour of the successful party.

In the event of no party receiving an overall majority, a second deciding ballot between parties receiving more than 10% of votes would be held a week later. It was a very different system to the single ballot 'first past the post' method that Steven had been used to. Nevertheless, he had every confidence in its operation even though one of his friends had warned him about the 'total shambles of a system' he had personally encountered on his sole experience of a local French election due to poor organisation, a mountain of paperwork and the dodgy reputation of the eventual candidate elected as Mayor.

When polling Sunday arrived, they made their way straight after lunch to the local school to cast their votes. They took with them numbered voting cards that had been posted to them, together with their passports. After walking across the school yard, they were greeted at the polling station door by a police officer and asked to produce their documentation. After careful inspection he waved them cheerfully through. So far, so good.

They joined a short queue and eventually presented the same documents to a lady clerk who then attempted to find their names on the voters register. Five minutes and several questions later, she had not been able to locate them. She called for assistance from a scrutineer but he too perused the long lists of names without success. He concluded that if the names of Steven and Joyce could not be located, they must not be on the list and could not vote! They stood their ground, insisting that they were formally registered and had personally confirmed that fact in one of the candidate's office a few days previously. A third official arrived. After phone calls to unknown people who, unusually for France must have been working on a Sunday, he triumphantly announced, Inspector Clouseau style, that being of British nationality, their names had been placed not on the local residents list but on the European voters list. *Voila!*

The lady clerk they had first spoken to then searched frantically for the European list but without avail. Further time elapsed before she returned somewhat embarrassed holding a single sheet of paper. She explained with a nervous laugh that this was the European list that had somehow been 'borrowed' by one of the candidates! It contained only eight names of which Steven and Joyce were numbers one and two.

Their eligibility to vote finally established and signatures obtained against their names on the European list, they were each given an envelope and seven different coloured pieces of paper, replicas of the ones they had already received in the post! Clearly, most voters do not bring their posted copies with them! They were instructed to separately enter a voting booth, pull the curtain across, select the paper of the party for whom they wished to vote, place it in the envelope and turn down the flap. The remaining six papers would then be surplus to requirements and could be disposed of. Most voters discarded the six unwanted papers on the floor of the voting booth and inevitably it was knee deep in litter.

Coming out of the booth with her envelope, Joyce was directed towards a queue leading to two scrutineers and a gentleman sitting behind a transparent glass ballot box. The reason for the queue was the cumbersome method of dealing with each voter. First, one of the scrutineers requested her voting card, identity card or passport, demanded verification of address and then a signature in the first box against her name on the scrutineers list. Then, moving slowly forward towards the gentleman, he took the envelope from her, rose to his feet and placed it slowly and deliberately in the slot in the top of the box. Only then did he pull a lever to allow the envelope to drop, when a bell rang (ting). He accompanied his action with the loud authoritative exclamation *'You have voted'*. He repeated the same procedure with Steven. It was all so theatrical but added some amusement to what was supposed to be the serious business of choosing a council and mayor.

On their way home, Steven remarked to Joyce that in some respects, his friend's comments about the procedure being 'a bit of a shambles' had proved to be correct. They justified it as being 'the French way'.

Late that evening the results were announced. Of the seven parties, those of the 'THE RAT' with 45% and of *M. Andre-Xavier Echeverrie* (commonly known in the French manner by his initials, AXE) with 41%, secured more than the required votes to be eligible for the next round. The remaining votes were divided among the five other parties, none of whom received the required 10% and were accordingly eliminated.

2

At this juncture, it is necessary to go back twenty years for the full flavour of the story. At that time, the current Mayor was one *M. Henri Lachance*, a highly decorated *(Légion d'Honneur, Chevalier de L'Ordre National du Mérité* and all that) local politician with fingers in most political pies. He retained his position as mayor of the town for seventeen years until his sudden death in office. How he retained power for such a long, unbroken period was quite astonishing. In an attempt to promote ambitious projects to rejuvenate the town's economy, he was at the forefront of a proposal to construct an International standard 60,000 seat sports stadium. The justification for such a large stadium with a capacity exceeding the town's population is unknown, but somehow the project was approved and millions of *francs* entrusted to a private developer. Unable to believe his good fortune, the developer, as developers are often prone to do, naturally fled with the funding. Not only fled, but disposed of the lot before being apprehended. The Mayor, adept as mayors are at spending other people's money, naturally bore no personal responsibility. Bonnetocque residents were left to repay the loss through imposition of increased local taxes.

If you have followed the story so far, you will be perfectly entitled to ask about the controls exercised that should have helped avoid this sort of abuse of public funding. Should not the permanent officers of the council have advised the Mayor against such a naive practice? Were there not rules regulating the council's cash management activities? The civil servant in charge of a *sous-préfecture* such as Bonnetocque is the S*ous-Préfect* assisted by a general secretary. *Sous-préfects* are usually skilled, hard-working individuals chosen from civil administrators assigned to the Ministry of the Interior. However, and this would appear to be the flaw, they are rarely in the same job for more than three years and can be immediately posted to other positions anywhere in France. Without continuity, the scope for bad practice and, as in this case ultimate fraud, is enhanced. And what of the opposition? Were they not monitoring what was going on or were they a small voice lost in the almost total power the Mayor and his party obtain as a result of the electoral allocation of seats? More of that later.

On the basis of 'you **can** fool most of the people all of the time', *M. Henri Lachance* continued to be returned to power until his death. With three years of his mayoralty to run, the favourite to succeed was his daughter *Marylise Lachance,* for ten years a local councillor, her father's confidant and virtual deputy (or to use that lovely French description, *Dauphine*) in waiting.

Marylise alas, was nothing like the image of a regal beauty the description *Dauphine* may conjure up. In reality, she was a large, pale, fat faced, middle aged woman who looked as though she had never done a hard days work in her life. A typical leech-type politician, her podgy fingers and long manicured nails were adept at attaching themselves to the political structures of society and sucking the lifeblood from a long-suffering public to her own personal benefit. Steven and Joyce had experienced the dubious pleasure of her company when, at a celebratory annual dinner in a local area of town, a mix-up over seating arrangements found them eventually sat next to the entourage of *Marylise Lachance.* As the conversation inevitably turned to politics, they discovered that when a question of policy arose, she turned to her willing acolytes who were only too eager to supply a ready answer. They found her to be a competent conveyor of received information, but certainly no intellectual. Upon the arrival of the *'confit de canard'* (leg of duck) main course, she declared herself to be a vegitarian and proceeded to consume a large plate of goats cheese salad followed by four slices of apple tart. Suitable fodder for such a woman.

She fought hard for elevation but the ultra conservatives within the party wanted change. The eventual outcome was the choice of 'THE RAT', a lawyer regarded at that time as a sound and competent politician. The two publicly buried their differences. *Marylise Lachance* was named as *Dauphine* to 'THE RAT'. They continued in office until the next election. All seemed sweetness and light when 'THE RAT' was retained as head of the Conservative group with *Marylise* confirmed as his loyal second in command.

3

We now fast forward to the second round of the election a week after the first.

With opinion polls predicting the result 'too close to call', the deciding ballot was held. The procedure was as before but this time with only two parties headed by 'THE RAT' and AXE.

In appearance and personality, the two could not have been more different. 'THE RAT' presented as a tall, portly figure in his late sixties, with a round, rosy cheeked face and a mane of fine, wispy, white hair. For his age and weight, he walked with an upright, confident stride and was usually seen casually dressed in an expensive, if well-worn suit and an open-necked shirt. His amiable features conveyed an avuncular air giving the impression of one who had seen it all before and readily knew what to do. In public, he was absolutely charming and far removed from his sobriquet. He was seen frequently dining in local cafés and restaurants, enjoying his *magret de canard*. But beneath the veneer there lurked a cunning and devious mind.

AXE on the other hand was of small stature accentuated by a crouching stance that transmitted the vague feeling of uncertainty and hesitancy to the observer. Slightly built, his receding hair line, thin lips, grey, pencil-like moustache, worried looking face and furrowed brow, gave him the appearance of being much older than his fifty-five years. Politically however, Steven and Joyce were to find out that there was much more to him than met the eye.

Once again, Steven and Joyce went to vote and had no problem this time in establishing their names on the list. They gave their necessary proofs of identity, signed in the second box next to their signatures of the previous week and saw their voting envelope enter the sealed ballot box, laughing again at the largely ceremonial cry of *'You have voted'*.

Like his friend, Steven also considered that it was an administratively top heavy and painfully slow system but concluded that there seemed to be more than sufficient checks and verifications to ensure complete integrity of 'one man, one vote'.

This time, the Conservative Party of 'THE RAT' gained 12,000 votes (for simplicity, the numbers are rounded) and the Socialist Party of AXE, 11,900, a difference of a mere 100 votes. Scrutiny of the papers next morning revealed that a batch of 25 votes for AXE had erroneously been accorded to 'THE RAT'. The difference was thus reduced to 50 votes. Easily done but sloppy, thought Steven.

AXE's team had also been checking the records. They soon revealed such a catalogue of errors that within two weeks, AXE had filed complaints to the High Court alleging gross electoral irregularities by 'THE RAT'. As enquiries were undertaken, 'THE RAT' retained his position as Mayor of Bonnetocque.

It was soon determined that an additional 400 proxy votes had been recorded on the second ballot (from 600 to 1,000); there were striking dissimilarities in signatures from one week to the next on a number of votes; and several more instances giving rise to charges of 'signature forgery'. Many people living in elderly peoples homes were noted to have somehow voted in the second round but not in the first.

Evidence was provided of incentives given to residents whereby they would obtain council jobs, housing or lucrative contracts in return for supporting 'THE RAT'.

Eight people were understood to have facilitated these events, including a number of police officers. The Inspector General of Police, whose role it is to 'police the police', later found that several officers had indeed committed irregularities in preparing proxy votes between the two rounds. The 'RATS' chauffeur was indicted and one of his relatives admitted to having written a number of proxies without those persons knowledge. Several signatures had been forged including those of a person on holiday at the time and a soldier on military duty overseas. The defence of those accused was that they had completed paperwork *only to facilitate administrative procedures*!! AXE's claim that 'THE RAT' had conducted a system of organised electoral fraud generated public concern over exactly who was the brain behind such surreptitious ploys.

As politicians do, 'THE RAT' totally rejected the accusations and countered by filing complaints against AXE for 'embezzlement' and 'vote buying'. His insinuations were that someone claiming to be the 'Director General of External Security' witnessed 'about a dozen youths' receiving envelopes from a 'middle man'. Moments later he had interviewed one of the youths who had complained that he had only received €100 whereas the others had got €150! He gave what was said to be a precise description of the 'middle man' as a man with greying hair, wearing a three-quarter dark brown coat, a grey cap and a red scarf. This would match the description of the several people in Bonnetocque who are regularly let out on a Wednesday afternoon!

Within six months, grievances were before an investigating judge. This resulted in the Council of State annulling the elections, citing that various 'manoeuvres' had altered the sincerity of the ballot.

A further election was scheduled for later in the year when, despite unresolved allegations of serious irregularities, both 'THE RAT' and AXE had no hesitation in once again heading the two main parties. This time *Marylise Lachance* decided to distance herself from the accusations against 'THE RAT', did not appear on his list and took no part in the election.

In a reversal of previous results, AXE polled a first round 48% of the vote, 'THE RAT' 36% and three further parties a mere 16% in total. The deciding election between the two protagonists saw AXE triumph and replace 'THE RAT' as Mayor of Bonnetocque.

4

With that, you might justifiably conclude, with investigations proceeding against him, 'THE RAT's political career was at an end. Indicted for complicity in 'false administration and use'; complicity of 'corruption to improper exercise of proxy voting'; 'damage to the sincerity of the vote', and 'serious violations of most basic democracy,' he appeared to have suffered total humiliation.
On the contrary. He continued as leader of the opposition. As investigations against him proceeded almost to the point of stagnation, he must have been hopeful when, upon hearing that the regional prosecutor had been told by superiors to be 'rid of this embarrassing hot potato,' that it might be swept under the carpet and consigned to history.

But behind the scenes, it slowly and quietly continued. Five years elapsed following this confusion before the examining magistrate decided to refer seven people, including 'THE RAT' to correctional court. The outcome failed to establish 'THE RAT's practical involvement in the organisation of fraud. He received a rap on the knuckles but his underlings were made to pay the price.
This judgement will come as little surprise to readers who will recall that sharks never attack lawyers because they see each other as kin and lawyers tend to look after their own in the same paternal way.

They interpret the rules, are best placed to know just what they can get away with and upon whom to deflect the blame.

To redress the balance, it wasn't long before a further hearing conducted by a judge concluded that his investigations had also failed to establish 'THE RAT's' claims that AXE had bribed members of the public to vote for him.
I feel that you will agree that it was a spurious contention for if you think it through, it would require several things to happen. You would need someone to provide the money.Then sufficient people, not just 'a dozen youths' as claimed, willing to accept it, promise to vote for you and keep quiet about it. Finally, you would have to trust them to do so. Two hundred people at least would be required to make a significant difference. At €150 each the cost would be €30,000.
It was later claimed that the mysterious 'middle man' wearing the distinctive attire had been recognised as one of AXE's 'assessors', although never identified. I don't think the police would have wasted much time searching for him but perhaps 'THE RAT' should have additionally been charged with wasting the courts time?

5

Whilst all this was going on, AXE had taken up his post as Mayor of Bonnetocque at a personal salary of €35,000 per annum and initially proved to be surprisingly impressive. Taking delight in his success and new role, for the first two years, he was seen regularly, speaking authoritatively at meetings, displaying a deep understanding of his home town's history and mapping out plans for its future needs. New initiatives to help citizens, such as free local transport and Christmas gifts for the elderly, free pop concerts for the young and increased expenditure aimed at increasing tourism, were introduced.
You will recall that Steven and Joyce had found local rates to be expensive and, like them, you will have been quick to realise that all the initiatives mentioned above would tend to increase them even more. With hindsight, AXE would also have to admit that such policies contributed to his eventual downfall. But, at that juncture, why should he care? Such free spending was popular with the less

well off people who had voted him in and if things did eventually get out of hand, he bore no personal responsibility.

He basked in his newly acquired power. Steven and Joyce often saw him near his home in the centre of town, always accompanied by his faithful companion, a friendly black Labrador. It would be true to say, that being French and proud to be the leading dog owners in Europe, most citizens of the town preferred to pat the dogs head than shake the hand of its owner. By the same token most would have admitted preferring to vote for the faithful, trustworthy Labrador rather than its master. Nonetheless, the dogs popularity was all to the benefit of AXE.

Then, just as suddenly as he had appeared to be a breath of fresh air upon the local political scene, AXE and his dog disappeared from it. For the next three years, he was rarely seen. Steven and Joyce thought he must have been demoted as, when his name did occasionally appear in the media, it referred to him as *Monsieur Député Maire*. Not so. He was still officially Mayor of Bonnetocque but also, as a député in the National Assembly, this was his preferred title. Steven and Joyce were soon to realise why. With a yearly income exceeding €150,000, free first class travel and flights; cheap housing loans, phone calls and postage, not to mention the gold-plated pension scheme, it was no wonder that representatives preferred the title *'député maire'*, one they are entitled to use for the rest of their lives, even after losing their seat. AXE clearly had his priorities right. As a passenger on the national gravy train, why would he want to bother too much about his apparently secure position as Mayor of Bonnetocque where his main opposition was divided and still under investigation for fraud?

In his absence, the town and its residents suffered. The already dilapidated pavements fell into further disrepair; footpaths and roads subjected to heavy winter snowfalls displayed deep potholes; business closures resulted in many empty shops. The town centre acquired a run down appearance, frequented by tramps, beggars, drug users and people of no fixed abode. Litter of all descriptions became an ever-increasing problem and the whole place had a downtrodden, neglected look.

As the next election date approached, unexpected events started to happen. AXE reappeared upon the scene, alas without his dog, but full of energetic promise to put the town in order. Local newspapers carried lists of plans quickly approved for immediate implementation. For several weeks, various parts of the town centre were disrupted so that footpaths and highways could be repaired; 'sleeping policemen' and speed recorders installed to enhance road safety and tubs of flowers introduced within pedestrian areas. Unfortunately, this piecemeal drive to obtain last minute votes was uncoordinated. Teams of men arriving with heavy equipment to resurface roads found that they had not been cordoned off. Owners of parked cars could not be traced. The work went ahead with the finished product looking like a patchwork quilt with many unimproved rectangular areas where tarmac-laying machines had skirted around parked cars.

6

His name now cleared over the previous election scandal, 'THE RAT' assumed his position as leader of the Conservative opposition to be safe. He was now free to convert that role once again into Mayor of Bonnetocque. But, with the two main protagonists having having spent much time trying to counter the allegations hovering over them, *Maryline Lachance* had been conspiring behind the scenes in Paris. Profiting from the distrust encompassing 'THE RAT,' this ambitious, devious, woman finally achieved her objective of being chosen by the national commission of the Conservative party to replace him as their candidate in the forthcoming Bonnetocque election.
Deprived of national party support, it appeared to be the final nail in the coffin of 'THE RAT's' political ambitions.

As the election approached Steven and Joyce were faced with the prospect of choosing between five teams of candidates including the parties of AXE, the National Front and *Maryline Lachance.*

Disillusioned both by the performance of the left wing National government and AXE's inactivity during his mayoralty, opinion polls showed him in third place, well behind *Maryline Lachance* and a resurgent National Front.

That information galvanised 'THE RAT' into action. He suspected that National Front support would be a protest not to be repeated on a second round of voting. If he did not oppose her, the treacherous *Maryline Lachance* would be a cast-iron certainty to sweep to victory and be elected mayor. A council member for over twenty years and mayor for three, it was a position he still coveted. Announcing that he was 'honour bound' to represent once again the 'vast number' of supporters who had begged him to stand, he put his name forward as leading candidate of the 'All for Bonnetocque' party. *Maryline Lachance* was furious and publicly invited him, unsuccessfully, to withdraw.
The now six competing party lists became seven when one of the smaller groups could not even agree among themselves. Their deputy broke away to form a further party.

Steven and Joyce once again found themselves choosing between seven competing parties. After five years when there had been more activity through the courts than there had been in Bonnetocque, four of the main candidates – AXE, National Front, 'THE RAT' and *Maryline Lachance* had been involved in the discredited aforementioned elections. Little had changed. The same old promises with the same old reckless speculators. In essence, a disparate group of people bound together by beguiling power, a drug that hooked them and a habit they were unable to kick. When Steven and Joyce had asked friends why decent, intelligent people had not come forward to oppose them, they were politely informed that honest citizens wished to remain that way and not become besmirched by the dirty world of politics! Once in power, politicians quickly adapted to the system and played it as profitably as they could. They became blind to their stated moral responsibilities, considering themselves to be always in the right and totally above the law.

So, in March, Steven and Joyce made their way to the school polling station, uncertain as to whom to support. 'THE RAT' and his long-time opponent AXE were both unworthy of their vote. National Front policies included discriminatory measures against foreigners and *Maryline Lachance* was hard to stomach. The two parties that emerged following disagreement were unattractive, leaving 'Long Live Bonnetocque', headed by an enthusiastic, middle-aged lady as the only party without a dubious past.

"Reading through the election pamphlets, it is impossible to distinguish between the parties. They all seem to promise the same things," observed Joyce. "We may as well vote for 'Long Live Bonnetocque' even though we know they will not be elected. We do know that whoever gets in will do very little for us."

With a list of mostly discredited candidates surrounded by suspicion and mistrust, it wasn't surprising that first round results were indecisive. AXE did manage to top the poll with 26%, ahead of National Front's 22%. To 'THE RAT's undisguised delight, his 'All for Bonnetocque' party wrested third place with 20% from the grasping *Maryline Lachance* on 18%.

Steven and Joyce were pleased to see their nice, middle-aged lady secure 8% and save her deposit. The folly of the other two parties was underlined when both failed to secure state funding to which they would have been entitled if they had remained as one.

A *quadrangulaire* election beckoned with each party with over 10% progressing to the final poll.

7

Two days later, a sudden shift occurred in the attitudes of both 'THE RAT' and *Maryline Lachance*, reported by the French press in their halting English translation: -

'Maximillion Ratti / Maryline Lachance, the merger is signed'
They have come in from their tinkering. Failure to solemnise a marriage of love, the centre-right look forward to a marriage of convenience. They are in this sacred union, forced by their near parity scores. The two parties have legitimate reasons for hope to lead the two love birds together in their new romance. Lachance has

said, "Maximillion, you won the primary, you are mayor in waiting". The two families found themselves formalising the marriage.'

In other words, opportunism ruled. The deciding election would be a *triangulaire* affair with the 'marriage' aiming to squeeze the vote of the other two parties.
Both AXE and the National Front candidate forcibly expressed indignation and anger. The marriage of 'the rodent and the scared rabbit' was just one of several choice accusations that can be printed. The two collaborators were unmoved. Their pact was perfectly legal and as the saying goes, there has always been honour among thieves.

'THE RAT', now as Conservative party leader, tried to deflect criticism by taking a statesman-like position, speaking eloquently of saving the town's faltering finances by the application of Keynesian supply and demand principles. In the general hubbub, few recalled that having said the same thing when he was mayor, his Keynesian interpretation then was '*I will demand, the ratepayers will supply*'.

Following the election, when Steven and Joyce reluctantly cast their votes for AXE, who had received the recommendation of their nice, middle-aged lady, the result was long delayed, indicating a very close poll. Eventually, after two recounts, it was announced in reverse order: -

Party	%	Votes
National Front	19.6	4,700
AXE	39.6	9,500
'THE RAT'	40.8	9,800

Victory for 'THE RAT' and his unholy alliance by just 300 votes.

For a man who, throughout the five years of judicial review of his involvement in complicity to influence elections, 'THE RAT's approach had proved to be masterly. He admitted nothing and directed the blame elsewhere. Despite, as captain of the ship being caught asleep at the wheel, his minions were found to have tinkered with and corrupted the democratic system, while he was left free to sail on to an improbable victory. Proof if any were needed that every cloud has a silver lining!

It is worth recording, in this modern democratic age, that there were over 1,200 spoilt votes (electors who protested by placing either a blank or defaced paper in their envelop) and a significant abstention rate of 34%. The winner received only 26% of all eligible votes. It is often said that if you don't vote you can't complain.This of course is not the fault of democracy but the electorate's disillusionment with the type of candidates and promises presented to them. With participation falling to a point where just a few votes can make a difference then the attraction of compulsory voting is increasingly discussed. Whether or not that would make any difference is debatable. The main parties with their organisation and spending power have a huge advantage over anyone trying to break the mould.The example of Bonnetocque points to the need for firm administrative controls backed by resolute application of the law and change in the method of awarding seats.

On the latter point, the French have a weird and wonderful system of allocating seats to the parties of their councils.
With 47 seats available in Bonnetocque, the successful party receive an initial 24 to ensure an overall majority.The remaining 23 are allocated proportionally among all the parties, *including the party that has already received the majority bonus,* according to the number of votes achieved in relation to the overall total of valid votes.
Having calculated the quotas, 'THE RAT' received 33 seats, AXE 9 and National Front 5.
Thus, the opposition, despite polling 59% of the votes acquired less than 30% of the seats, hardly proportional and unrepresentative of the local population's wishes. It does however give the winning party, even one successful by a few votes, absolute power to brush aside any opposition views. As we has seen, this can lead to projects being approved with very little planning or control, often to the detriment of

the electorate who have to pick up the bill. When politicians simply increase taxes to cover their capricious schemes, what alternative does the voter have? This standard ploy usually breeds distrust, resentment, strikes (at which the French are undisputed world champions) and lawlessness leading to political disorder.

8

A week later 'THE RAT, as leader of the largest party, presided over the first meeting of the new council and immediately declared himself a candidate for election as Mayor.

AXE was conspicuous by his absence and it fell to a spokesman to express his contempt at what he described as the 'despicable and totally dishonourable marriage of convenience' that had brought shame on the town and sullied the democratic process.

The National Front candidate demanded to be heard. Looking, steely-eyed, directly at 'THE RAT,' he declared his 'no confidence' in him and proposed himself for the post of Mayor. 'THE RAT,' who reminded him, to some derisive laughter, that he should remember that he was part of a democracy and must abide by the rules, mocked him. As one opposition member, anticipating future conflict within the council chamber was overheard to suggest, 'perhaps our solution is dissolution before we have another revolution'?

Members were invited to vote for the election of Mayor. With 33 votes for, 5 against and 8 abstentions, 'THE RAT', rising bold as brass to be draped by *Maryline Lachance* with the tri-colour sash of office, was elected to power as Mayor of Bonnetocque for six more years. *Plus ça change, plus c'est la même chose!*

Next day, as Steven and Joyce walked down by the river, Steven noticed that there appeared to be fewer ducks than normal. He wondered that perhaps they too, like Bonnetocque local elections, were not as watertight as had been thought. Not that *that* could be blamed on *Marylise Lachance*, more the fault of 'THE RAT'.

Often, the truth is stranger than fiction.

JAMES FRANKLYN JACKSON

Born in the North of England in 1943, the original intention of naming him in honour of United States President *Franklin Delano Roosevelt* was thwarted due to a typographical error on the part of the registrar when the 'i' became 'y'.

Reared, due to wartime food shortages on a diet of semolina and later, football and cricket, he went on to waste five years at the local grammar school. Having no perception of what the future might hold, he stumbled into local government, eventually obtaining an accountancy qualification and an OU degree. There followed thirty-five largely undistinguished years that at least encouraged his interest in ceremonial procedures and customs.

Taking early retirement and still seeking his true role in life, he was fortunate to find it first of all as a civil servant and then a consultant, both overseas - but these are other stories.

Finally settling in France, he has experienced their wonderful lifestyle particularly food and drink about which you will find many examples. Their often eccentric local administrative systems have been observed and suffered with more than a passing interest.
A writer of many long forgotten reports for sundry committees, his later reading includes an appreciation of short stories, particularly those of his favourite, Guy de Maupassant.

All characters and situations in these stories are essentially true. Any relationship to fictitious people or imaginary happenings is coincidental. Only the names have been changed to protect the innocent or in a number of cases, the guilty.

If you think you recognise one or more of the characters and would like to contact him (jfj112@hotmail.com), please understand that credit has been awarded where merited and hostile expressions of opinion made upon those whom the writer thinks deserve them. He takes no responsibility for what you might consider to be errors or omissions.